STILL LIFE *with* MURDER

"P.B. Ryan makes a stunning debut with *Still Life with Murder,* bringing nineteenth century Boston alive, from its teeming slums to the mansions on Boston Common, and populating it with a vivid and memorable cast of characters. The fascinating heroine, Nell Sweeney, immediately engages the reader and I couldn't put the book down until I discovered the truth along with her. I can't wait for the next installment."

—Bestselling author Victoria Thompson

"What a thoroughly charming book! A beautiful combination of entertaining characters, minute historical research, and a powerful evocation of time and place. I'm very glad there will be more to come."

—*New York Times* bestselling author Barbara Hambly

"P.B. Ryan captures an authentic flavor of post-Civil War Boston as she explores that city's dark underbelly and the lingering after-effects of the war. The atmosphere is that of *The Alienist,* but feisty Irish nursemaid Nell Sweeney is a more likable protagonist. I look forward to seeing her in action again."

—*New York Times* bestselling author Rhys Bowen

MURDER *in* A MILL TOWN

DEATH *on* BEACON HILL

"I decided to start the year off with my favorite mystery series. The mystery itself—what really happened that afternoon at Mrs. Kimball's and who killed her and her maid—kept me guessing....Highly recommend the series."

—Babbling Book Reviews

"*Death on Beacon Hill* continues Ms. Ryan's excellent Nell Sweeney series. The rich characterization and her strong evocation of place, coupled with a well-plotted tale, make for a rich story. Add a clever conclusion and Ms. Ryan delivers a fascinating read."

—Fresh Fiction

"[Nell is] intelligent and has a strong sense of justice....She only takes action after careful consideration, never rushing to throw herself in harm's way....They mystery consists of several layers, and is constructed quite well....It's clear from the beginning that things are not as they seem; this serves to keep the reader interested in ferreting out the clues alongside Nell. I'm looking forward to another installment."

—The Romance Reader's Connection

MURDER *on* BLACK FRIDAY

"A mesmerizing mystery. Not only does Ryan provide readers with a tightly wound, suspenseful novel peopled with multidimensional characters, she writes about an era whose problems mirror our own. This is a historical period she knows and brings to life so clearly that readers are totally immersed. Nell is an ideal heroine: smart, intrepid and human. Be on the lookout for her return."

—RT BookReviews

"Nell and Will are a confirmed pair of amateur sleuths in this fourth entry in the popular Gilded Age series, and this makes the setting perhaps slightly cozier, but as usual, P B Ryan is spot on with her period detail. This is the best part about the series for me, as these books really do open a window into how both the high and low society of Boston operated. She thankfully doesn't shrink (Anne Perry style) from showing it, warts and all…probably the best entry yet."

—MyShelf.com

"As always, Nell and Will's predicament tugs at my heart. Loved it!"

—Babbling Book Reviews

"The author has an amazing grasp of life during this period of history. Each detail is crafted to let the reader feel immersed in the time; from the major historical events, to the minutiae of everyday life. These facts are effortlessly woven into the overall narrative."

—The Romance Reader's Connection

MURDER *in the* NORTH END

"This is the latest in a unique and enjoyable series. The necessary background is easily dispensed with, making it easy for newcomer and longtime reader alike. The author uses the historical period to great advantage, depicting the class separations and prejudices that existed at the time without romanticizing them. Nell and Will are both fascinating characters. From wholly disparate backgrounds, they should have no common ground. But they each have past pains and secrets that allow them to understand each other. They make a great sleuthing team, as well. It's always a good day when a new Nell Sweeney book arrives."

—*CA Reviews*

"Plucky Nell and her helpmate Will are well developed characters who are likeable and smart. The cast of supporting characters in this book is colorful and well drawn, making the book an easy read. All of the books in this series are enjoyable; *Murder in the North End* is no exception.... I eagerly await the next Gilded Age mystery."

—*Cozy Library*

"*Murder in the North End* is a light read that you can cozy up to on a cold winter night in your easy chair by the fire..."

—*MyShelf.com*

MURDER *in the* NORTH END

The Nell Sweeney Mysteries by P.B. Ryan

Still Life with Murder

Murder in a Mill Town

Death on Beacon Hill

Murder on Black Friday

Murder in the North End

A Bucket of Ashes

Medieval Romantic Suspense by Patricia Ryan

Falcon's Fire

Heaven's Fire

Secret Thunder

Wild Wind

Silken Threads

The Sun and the Moon

Contemporary Women's Fiction by Patricia Ryan

Pure and Simple

Hale's Point

A Burning Touch

Non-fiction by Patricia Ryan, aka P.B. Ryan

Writing the Novel They Can't Put Down

MURDER
in the
NORTH END

❧ ❧

P.B. Ryan

Copyright © 2006 Patricia Burford Ryan

A Hawkley Books Trade Paperback

A mass market paperback edition of this book was published in 2006 by Berkley Prime Crime.

An electronic edition was published in 2010 by Hawkley Books.

The cover art is *The Orchestra Pit, Old Proctor's Fifth Avenue Theater* by Everett Shinn, 1906.

ISBN: 0692217533
ISBN 13: 9780692217535

CHAPTER ONE

July 1870: Boston

"M ORE TEA, LADY HIGGINBOTTOM?" ASKED Nell Sweeney, sitting Indian-style beneath a sheet arranged over four dainty little gilt chairs.

"I don't mind if I do," Gracie responded in her best attempt at an upper-crust English drawl. The five-year-old offered her tiny cup to be filled with imaginary tea from the little gold-rimmed bone china teapot in her governess's hand. "And a spot of cweam, if you don't mind? *Cream,*" Gracie corrected before Nell had a chance to do it for her. Her diction, thankfully, had seen major improvements over the past few months.

"More for you, Lady Wigglesworth?" Nell asked as she turned to her young assistant, Eileen Tierney.

"I shouldn't, but I don't suppose another sip or two would hurt," said the waifish, flaxen-haired Eileen as she held out her cup. Her own attempt to sound like a British aristocrat was rather less successful than Gracie's, due mainly to an Irish brogue far too deeply ingrained to disguise. "Aye, and this here's the perfect mornin' for a tea party, it is. Yes, indeed. What ho. Cheers, and all that."

"Another drop, Lord Hubble-Bubble?" Nell proffered the teapot to Gracie's little red poodle, Clancy, who sniffed curiously as she tilted it over his cup.

"I say, Hitchens, have you seen the Sweeney girl?"

The clipped inquiry, which came from beyond their little makeshift tent, prompted grimaces from Nell's tea party companions. Even Clancy let out a weary little sigh.

"Mrs. Mott," Gracie mouthed with a theatrical expression of repugnance.

From the nearness of the housekeeper's voice, Nell realized she must have crept right into the third-floor nursery on those silent-as-death feet of hers. Edward Hitchens, Mr. Hewitt's valet, was probably passing outside in the hall.

Nell was about to announce her presence when Mrs. Mott added, in a tone of hushed significance, "There's a constable downstairs, asking for her."

Hitchens responded to this news with an eloquent little grunt. The starchy valet was the closest thing Evelyn Mott had to a confidant among the household staff. Like the dour old housekeeper, Hitchens was appalled at Nell's having supposedly finagled eccentric Viola Hewitt into hiring her as Gracie's nursery governess despite her humble origins and even worse, much worse, her Irishness. It mattered not that Nell blended flawlessly into the world of Brahmin privilege in which she lived and worked. She dressed like them, spoke like them, and comported herself like them, and with the exception of a slight coppery burnish to her hair, there was nothing overtly Gaelic in her appearance to give her away. Still, she was Irish, foreign vermin in the eyes of most Bostonians, lowborn or high.

"A *constable?*" Hitchen said. "Good lord. He didn't come to the front door, did he?"

"He did, indeed, just as bold as you please."

"God knows what the neighbors will think."

With a contemptuous little huff, Mrs. said, "God knows what they've been thinking for the past six years, with that Sweeney girl waltzing the child up and down Colonnade Row as if they belonged here. I've told Mrs. Hewitt it isn't fitting, but you know her—she just does as she pleases, with no regard for what people think, or how it reflects on Mr. Hewitt."

"Bad enough to take the child in," Hitchens sniffed, "but to raise her like one of the family, with an upstart Irisher looking after her instead of a proper governess..."

"It's not as if she merits a proper governess, but then, if she'd been correctly dealt with from the first, she'd be in the House of Industry instead of constantly underfoot here. I don't care if she *was* sired by a Hewitt, a chambermaid's by-blow has no business prancing about like a little princess under the roof of one of the best families in—"

"Mrs. Mott, is that you?" Nell called out as she belatedly realized, from Gracie and Eileen's puzzled scowls, that they'd heard far more than they should have. She was tired, having awakened well before sunrise to pack her and Gracie's luggage, or she would have put a halt to the conversation the moment she realized where it was going.

She folded back the sheet and stood, smoothing out the wrinkles in her traveling dress of brown summer-weight wool. "Ah, and Mr. Hitchens, too. How lovely of you to pay a call on us this morning—a rare treat. Would you care to join us?" she asked, holding up the diminutive teapot.

The housekeeper and valet blinked at her from the doorway of the nursery, an opulent bower fitted out with child-sized rococo-inspired furniture swathed entirely, as of yesterday, in snowy linen sheets. Hitchens turned and left in stony silence, leaving Mrs. Mott to frown at Gracie and Eileen as they clambered to their feet.

Stiffening her back, her hands clasped at her waist, the housekeeper said to Nell, "Your presence is required downstairs. There is a Constable Skinner waiting to speak with you in the music room."

Skinner. That ghastly little weasel. What on Earth could he be wanting with her?

Nell suspected she knew why Mrs. Mott had had him sequestered in the music room instead of the front parlor, as was customary. The parlor, which looked out onto the elegant stretch of Tremont Street known as Colonnade Row, had numerous tall windows, all of which would be thrown wide open with their curtains tied back on this sultry summer morning. The music room, on the other hand, faced a little-used side street. Even with its windows uncurtained, there would be few passersby to notice a policeman paying a visit to the venerable Hewitts.

"I'll be down shortly," Nell said.

"Do expedite your business with this…gentleman," said Mrs. Mott. "It is imperative that we all be ready to leave promptly at ten o'clock. That's less than an hour from—"

"Our bags are all packed and in the entrance hall," Nell said. "We just thought we'd enjoy a spot of tea before our trip."

Gracie lifted her empty tiny cup toward the housekeeper as if in a toast, and brought it to her lips. Mrs. Mott fixed the little girl with a nostril-flaring grimace before stalking away.

"Miseeney," Gracie asked as she crouched down to gather Clancy in her arms, "what's a by-blow?"

Eileen looked at Nell, her bottom lip caught in her teeth. She clearly *did* know what a by-blow was, even if she didn't know, or hadn't until now, that Viola Hewitt's adopted daughter was the illegitimate child of one of her own servants. Viola had long ago forbidden the household staff to speak of Gracie's origins, although clearly Mrs. Mott and Hitchens felt themselves above such constraints. As far as Gracie knew, her Nana had picked her out special after bringing up four sons because she'd always longed for a daughter.

"A by-blow..." Nell began hesitantly. She smoothed a hand over Gracie's plaited and beribboned hair, as black and glossy as that of her father. "It's a silly word for a child. It doesn't mean anything."

The little girl nodded uncertainly as she nuzzled the little dog, who responded by licking her chin. "What's the House of Industwy?" Gracie was at the age where, once the questions started, they just kept coming.

Eileen looked at Nell as if wondering how she was going to answer that one.

Nell said, "It's...a big house on a place called Deer Island where people go to live." A house for paupers, orphans, the mad and diseased and doomed—a place not unlike the Barnstable County Poor House, where Nell had spent much of her dismal youth.

"It's on an island?" Gracie asked, bobbing up and down as she did when she was excited. "Can we go live there after you and Uncle Will get mawwied? *Married?*"

"Umm..."

Nell's sham courtship with the Hewitts' eldest son, William, was a fiction intended to facilitate his spending time with her and Gracie without arousing unseemly whispers. Will had proposed the ruse last summer in order to silence speculation that the prim and proper young governess might be carrying on with the notorious surgeon-turned-gambler who was the black sheep of the Hewitt family. If they were thought to be unofficially engaged, Will reasoned, no one would question their friendship.

It was a friendship that could never amount to more, given that *Miss* Nell Sweeney was, in fact, already married to an inmate at Charlestown State Prison. Duncan, whom she hadn't seen in two years, was currently ten years into a thirty year sentence for armed robbery and aggravated assault. The only people in Boston who knew about him, and the rest of her questionable past, were Will and Father Gorman at St. Stephen's, who served as her confessor. They were the only people who must ever know, lest she torn away from this charmed life and the child she'd come to love as her own.

That child was now staring at her with her big, guileless eyes, waiting to find out whether she could take the place of a real daughter to the couple she'd grown to consider her surrogate parents. It was a question she'd asked a number of times since learning, no doubt through servants' careless comments, that Nell and Will were presumably destined to marry. This was the first time, however, that she'd proposed the county almshouse as their family home.

"We can't live at the House of Industry, buttercup," Nell answered, deliberately skirting the crux of the issue. "It's for people who don't have any other home. You've got a home here with Nana."

"But Nana's legs don't work. That's why she needs you." Clutching Clancy tight to her chest, the child gazed up at Nell with the exaggerated pathos of an actress in some tawdry melodrama. "I need you, too, Miseeney. Who will look after me if you aren't here?"

"What about Miss Tierney?" Nell asked.

"Aye, what about me?" Eileen demanded with pretended severity as she tweaked one of Gracie's braids.

"She could come, too, couldn't she? Please, Miseeney?" the child begged, hugging the dog tighter. *"Pleeease?"*

Nell crouched down so that they were at eye level and told her what she always ended up telling her. "Engagements can last a very long time, sweetie. It might be years before Uncle Will and I get married."

"But when you do, can I—"

"We'll settle that when the time comes."

"But—"

"I don't have time to discuss this right now." With a kiss on Gracie's forehead, Nell stood and said, "There's a constable downstairs who wants to speak with me, and one mustn't keep constables waiting. Why don't you and Miss Tierney make sure you haven't left anything behind that you want to bring to the Cape. I'll be back as soon as I can."

As she was leaving, Nell heard Gracie ask Eileen, "Miss Tiewny, what does 'sired' mean?"

"Er…"

"'Sired by a Hewitt,'" Gracie said. "What does that mean?"

Oh, hell. Pausing in the doorway, Nell said, "I'll explain it to you later," although she'd no notion of how she would wriggle out of that one.

NELL OPENED THE DOOR OF the music room to find Charlie Skinner standing with his back to her, lifting the sheet hanging over the largest of the many family portraits lining the rosewood paneled walls—a colossal full-length likeness of August Hewitt executed by his wife, Viola, a gifted amateur painter.

"You wanted to see me?" Nell asked as she closed the door behind her. Best not to let others be privy to their conversation, at least until she knew what in the devil he wanted with her.

Skinner turned, dropping the sheet, to address her with that look of vaguely amused disdain he seemed to reserve just for her. He hadn't changed much over the past year: same slight build and rodentlike features, although his prematurely salt-and-pepper hair had gotten noticeably grayer.

He surveyed her up and down with a trace of a sneer. "Miss *Sweeney.*" The emphasis on her Irish name was intended as an insult.

Giving tit for tat, Nell allowed herself a lingering appraisal of Skinner's attire, the dark blue uniform of the Boston constabulary.

A pair of handcuffs, a truncheon, and a holstered pistol hung on his belt; a policeman's hat sat on the sheet-draped grand piano.

"Constable," she said with a cool little smile. "It *is* 'Constable' now, not 'Detective?'"

Skinner's mouth compressed into a churlish slit. The last time Nell had seen him, over a year ago, he'd been wearing a sack suit and one of those gaudy plaid vests he was so inexplicably fond of. At the time, he'd been one of seven officers assigned to Boston's prestigious Detectives' Bureau headquartered at City Hall. In February, however, following a battery of hearings prompted by widespread police corruption, the Detectives' Bureau was abolished. Its members, save for a single detective who was found innocent of any major wrongdoing, were either sacked or downgraded to rank-and-file patrolmen. It would appear that Skinner had contrived to stay on as one of the demoted officers, but the reduction in rank had clearly stung.

From outside in the central hall came the thud of something heavy striking the marble floor, followed by a male voice hissing, "Shit!"

"You will watch your tongue in this house, young man." It was Mrs. Mott, in her shrill supervisory mode. "Pick up that trunk, you two. Come, come." She delivered two sharp claps. "You've not been hired to lollygag."

"It's bedlam out there," Skinner observed.

Indeed, a kind of semi-controlled chaos had gripped the Hewitts' Italianate mansion at dawn that morning, as twenty or so servants, aided by a fleet of hired cartmen, strove to transfer a vast array of household gear to the row of tipcarts and wagons clustered in the stable yard and lined up out front at the curb.

"The Hewitts spend most of July and August at Falconwood, their summer house on Cape Cod," Nell said. "We leave this morning."

"'We?' The servants, too?" he said.

The implication, that Nell was on the same level as the maids and footmen, wasn't lost on her. In fact, her status as governess put her in that shadowy borderline between the hired domestics and the family, a distinction that the constable surely recognized, but chose, in her case, to disregard.

"The entire staff travels with the family," she said. "The house will be closed up until the end of August."

Skinner made a show of looking around. "This big, swanky house standing empty for what—six, eight weeks? Aren't they afraid somebody might break in, make off with some of this fancy stuff?" He lifted the sheet over Viola's prized Limoges urn sitting on the piano.

"It happened a couple of years ago," Nell said. "Mr. Hewitt had stronger locks put on the doors."

"There's no lock so strong it can't be picked if you know how," Skinner said, reminding Nell the time Will had unlocked Virgil Hines's writing box with a flick of a hairpin. *You have a great many shameful talents, don't you?* she'd asked him.

"I could crack any lock in this house in less than a minute," the constable bragged.

"I'm all too sure you could," said Nell, who recalled that burglaries were among the infractions of which the disbanded detectives had been accused, in addition to rapes, extortion, bribery, murder for hire, and savage and unprovoked beatings of Irishmen and Negroes. "Did you come here just to chat, *Constable,* or is there a purpose to your visit?"

Crossing to the console table next to the door, Skinner uncovered a pair of Venetian lamps, very old and fragile. "There's been a murder in the North End. Local hood name of Johnny Cassidy took a bullet in the head last night in a concert saloon called Nabby's Inferno."

He picked up one of the lamps and held it aloft, turning it this way and that to watch the exquisite blue glass ignite in the sunlight from the open windows.

Carefully lifting the lamp from his hand, Nell set it back on the table and re-cloaked it with the sheet. "What happens in the North End is of no interest to me." Aside from the fact that it was home to tens of thousands of Irish, crammed together in their wretched waterfront hovels.

With a little snort of amusement, Skinner said, "Oh, yeah, you lace-curtain colleens think you're too good for that rat warren, don't you? Well, I happen to know you never miss early Sunday mass at St. Stephen's up on Hanover Street."

Rattled, but determined not to show it, Nell said, "Have you been spying on me, Constable?"

Skinner lifted the sheet draped over one of the six-foot obelisks flanking the entrance to the Red Room, Viola's private haven. "The North End is my beat—and us cops like to keep track of them that make trouble for us."

"I still don't see what the murder of a perfect stranger has to do with me."

"What it has to do with you," Skinner said as he strolled around the room, eyeing the shapes beneath the linen shrouds, "is that the murderer happens to be an old friend of yours." He met her gaze with a smug grin. "Detective Colin Cook."

CHAPTER TWO

❧

NELL SOMEHOW MANAGED TO KEEP her expression neutral even as her thoughts careened. Colin Cook, one of Skinner's former colleagues in the Detectives' Bureau, not that the rest of them had ever considered him as such, given his Irishness, had been the lone member of the bureau to escape the retribution meted out to the rest of them after the corruption hearings. Though not entirely blameless—Cook had been known to pocket a few greenbacks now and then—the bearlike black Irishman had enjoyed a singular reputation for integrity and competence. When the rest of the Boston detectives were fired or sent out to patrol the streets, Cook had been offered what amounted to a promotion: a coveted appointment to the Massachusetts State Constabulary. As a state detective, Cook was primarily charged with stemming Boston's rising tide of vice, although murder investigations also fell under his purview.

"I can't imagine that your information is correct," Nell said evenly, "if you've come to the conclusion that Detective Cook is the responsible party."

"You don't think he's capable of killing a man?"

"For just cause? Certainly. He fought for the Union, after all. But outright murder?" She shook her head. "I wouldn't expect the likes of you to understand such a thing, but there *are* men in this world who have moral standards, and Colin Cook is one of them."

"A pretty speech, Miss Sweeney," said Skinner with a mocking little bow, "and I'm sure if Cook were present to hear it, he'd be moved by your faith in him. But as it happens, that faith is sadly misplaced. He did do murder. He did it savagely, and I must say, rather sloppily. I was the first cop on the scene, and I can tell you it was pretty cut and dried. They all know him there—he's a regular—and we got three witnesses that say he done it."

"'We?' Surely you're not the officer handling this case. That would be the responsibility of the state detectives, would it not?"

"It would but for the fact that Major Jones, who's in charge of that unit, feels it would be a—what did he call it?—'conflict of interest' for his boys to investigate one of their own. Now, me, I've got experience as a detective, and no reason to want to go soft on Cook. So, in the interest of justice, I stepped forward and offered to—"

"In the interest of justice?" she scoffed. "In the interest of revenge, you mean. You'd like nothing more than to see Detective Cook hang."

Skinner tugged the sheet off the round marble table in the center of the room, laid out with a selection of August Hewitt's favorite antique musical instruments. He picked up the pocket hunting horn, a heavily coiled brass trumpet less than a foot long, dented and tarnished with age. Viola thought it ugly, and didn't see the point of keeping it out, but as the music room was her husband's special haven, the instrument remained on display.

Skinner hefted the horn as if testing its weight. "I won't deny that it gives me a warm feeling inside to see murderers twitch at the end of a noose."

Nell said, "It would give you no end of glee to see Detective Cook hang, if only because he's Irish, and a better man than you. But on top of that, he was actually rewarded when the truth came out about what you detectives were up to, while the rest of you ended up—"

"He sold us out," Skinner said, teeth bared. "He ratted on us in secret sessions during the hearings, just him and those big bugs that don't have the slightest idea what it takes to deal with the foreign vermin who've overrun this town. Next thing you know,

I end up policing Paddyland for a Paddy *captain,* of all damn things, who treats me like I'm some stray cat he'd like to drown, while that humbug-spouting mick gets bumped up to Jones's unit. He's earning almost twice what he used to, while I'm still making do on eight-hundred bucks a year."

"Surely, Constable, you're making the job pay better than that," Nell said with a knowing little smile.

In a crude imitation of an Irish accent, Skinner said, "Oh, you fancy yourself quite the clever little lass, don't you, now?"

"I'm not stupid," she said. "I know how you and your kind do business. As for Cook spouting humbug, what are you saying? Are you claiming he lied?"

"He made stuff up just to get us in hot water, and they swallowed it whole and asked for more."

"And how would you know that," she challenged, "if those sessions were so secret?"

"Oh, you *are* clever, aren't you?" He closed in on her, clutching her arm in a painful grip; she could smell the rum on his breath, the sour tang of his sweat. "You're two of a kind, you and Cook, a couple of crafty, high-reaching bogtrotters out to get what you can over the backs of all us regular, hardworking Americans. Yeah, but I'll bet you're not so high-and-mighty when the good detective gets you alone, eh? Do you give him a good ride, Miss Sweeney? Do you buck and scream and—"

"Get out." Nell tried to wrestle free of his grip, but she was no match for his wiry strength.

He slammed her one-handed against the door, holding her there as he tilted her chin up with the mouthpiece of the horn. In a menacing murmur he said, "I wouldn't mind hearing you scream."

"Nor I you." She wrenched the horn from his hand and whipped it across his face.

He stumbled back into the piano with a yowl of pain, his hands cupping his nose. "You *bitch!*" he screamed in a nasal rasp. "Jesus! You goddamned—"

"Get out." Nell opened the door to the hallway. Two kitchen maids passing by with armloads of pots and kettles paused to gape at the constable.

"I'm not going anywhere," he snarled as he advanced on her.

From the Red Room came a woman's steely, British-inflected voice. "Oh, I think you are."

Viola Hewitt, seated in her Merlin chair, wheeled herself through the doorway with an expression of resolute fury. Garbed with atypical severity in a tailored gray suit, her black-and-silver hair mostly concealed beneath a square-crowned riding hat trailing a swath of netting, Viola cut a daunting, almost majestic presence, even in the wheelchair.

Skinner stared unblinkingly at the revered Brahmin matron, blood trickling from between his fingers, before pointing a shaky finger at Nell. "She assaulted an officer of the law. I mean to have her brought up on—"

"And I mean to have you ejected from this house by my footmen, who will bloody more than your nose in the process, unless you leave here immediately."

Glaring at Nell, Skinner said, "I know you know where he is."

Nell said, "I have no idea what you're talking ab—"

"Cook." Skinner wiped his hand across his face, smearing it with blood; there was a livid scrape on his cheek, as well. "He disappeared last night, after shooting Cassidy. If anyone knows where he lit off to—"

"I haven't seen nor heard from Detective Cook in weeks," Nell said.

"You lying little—"

"Bridget," Viola said to one of the kitchen girls. "Would you fetch Peter and Dennis? I believe they're outside loading the—"

"I'm leaving," Skinner said, adding, to Nell, "Tell Cook we'll catch up with him sooner or later, and make no mistake, he *will* hang—I mean to make sure of it. As for you, don't you ever forget there are eyes out there, watching your every move. One of these days, Miss *Sweeney*, you're gonna get the lesson you've been begging for."

After he left, Viola nodded toward the brass horn still clutched tight in Nell's fist. "It's about time that hideous thing came in good for something."

Nell let out her breath in a tremulous chuckle. Viola cocked her head in the direction of the door, which Nell closed.

"Have a seat, my dear," said Viola as she wheeled further into the room. "You're white as chalk."

Nell sat on a sheet-swathed chair and rubbed her left arm, which was sore where Skinner had grabbed it.

"I realize I should have made my presence known," Viola said, "but curiosity overcame propriety when I caught on to the nature of the conversation, so I hid behind the curio cabinet. This Detective Cook, he's the one you're so fond of, yes?"

Nell sat back, nodding. "He's a good man, Mrs. Hewitt. I can't believe he'd murder someone. I *don't* believe it."

"Are you quite certain? Given the right situation, you might be surprised how brutal the nicest person can be."

Viola wouldn't be offering little insights on brutality if she knew what Nell's life had been like until about ten years ago. Choosing her words carefully, so as not to sound too conversant on the subject, Nell said, "It would seem to me that, to actually kill someone—not for just cause, but in anger, say—is to cross a line that most of us are incapable of crossing, no matter how enraged we become. It's as if God has equipped us with a sort of...moral brake that won't allow us to take a life unless there's an exceptionally good reason."

"Is it possible, do you suppose, that your Detective Cook might have felt that he had an exceptionally good reason to kill this...what was his name? Cassidy?"

"Johnny Cassidy. Something like self-defense, you mean? If that were the case, it must not be obvious, or else they wouldn't be hunting him down as a murderer."

"Nor," Viola pointed out gently, "would it be likely that he would have fled in the first place."

Nell closed her eyes and shook her head. "If you knew him as I know him..."

"Was it true, what you told Constable Skinner—that you haven't been in touch with Detective Cook?"

Nodding, Nell said, "The last time I saw him was two or three weeks ago. I'd taken Gracie for one of her afternoon outings in the Commons, and he passed by. We chatted for a while about the new house he'd just bought, and his work with the State Constabulary."

"He didn't mention anything about problems in the North End, or..."

"He did say he'd been spending quite a bit of time up there, in his professional capacity, which would stand to reason, given his current responsibilities. Fort Hill, too. The Irish slums are where most of the gaming dens and taverns and and...other such places are located."

"Brothels," Viola added with a smile. "You can say it—it's just us."

Nell returned her smile. One of the most Viola's most endearing qualities was her candor about such matters, a holdover from her early bohemian years in Paris.

"He mentioned his work," Nell said, "but only in a general way. He told me it was a big job, trying to stamp out vice in a city like Boston. He said that, by last count, there were over three-thousand places where liquor was sold, dozens of gaming halls, and somewhere between two and three-hundred…'houses of accommodation,' as he called them."

Viola chuckled at the euphemism.

Nell said, "If anyone could make inroads in cleaning up those neighborhoods, it would be Colin Cook. He's a very capable detective, and Irish, to boot. He fits in with those people, he knows how they think, he speaks their language. And he has a deeply ingrained sense of right and wrong."

"And yet," Viola said with a sigh, "he's now found himself a fugitive from the law."

Burying her face in her hands, still trembling from her encounter with Skinner, Nell said, "I can't imagine how this came to pass. It's not just Skinner who thinks he did it. The chief of the state constabulary must suspect him, else he wouldn't have ordered Skinner to track him down. I'm so afraid he's going to be found and…oh, God. By the time I come back from the Cape, he'll be in prison—if they haven't already hanged him by then. Who knows, Skinner might just take matters into his own hands and execute him on the spot, claiming he'd tried to make a break for it. I wouldn't put it past him."

Wheeling herself closer to Nell, Viola reached out to take her hand. "You want to help him, don't you?"

"How can I?" Nell asked shakily, her throat tightening with impending tears. "I'll…I'll be on the Cape while Skinner is hunting him down and…and…"

"And the whole while," Viola said, "you'll be fretting about your friend, wondering if he's been found."

"Or killed."

"I daresay you'll be no good to Gracie in such a state."

"No, I…I wouldn't let this interfere with—"

"You couldn't help it. You're only human." After a thoughtful pause, Viola said, "I know you. I know your sense of justice, your fidelity to your friends. You wish you were staying in Boston so that you could try to find your detective friend before Constable Skinner does."

"Of course, b-but—"

"You could, you know, if you wanted to."

Nell looked up. "Stay here? But—"

"For a while, anyway, until you'd sorted things out."

"But what about Gracie?"

"Eileen could look after her until you can join us on the Cape. I'll leave you money for the train. Just cable me at Falconwood to let me know when you'll be arriving at the Falmouth depot, and I'll send Brady to meet you. You see, it's really no great challenge to arrange—if it's really what you want."

"It is. But I would feel as if I were shirking my duty to Gracie…and to you."

"Gracie's adaptable, as am I. And Eileen is more than capable of shouldering the burden until you're back. The only question is where you would stay. I'm not sure I'm quite comfortable with you being all alone in this big, empty house. Do you have friends you could stay with?"

Nell sat back and thought about it. "There's Emily Pratt, but, well, she's still living in her parents' home until her marriage to Dr. Foster, and…"

"And it goes without saying that Orville Pratt wouldn't tolerate an Irish-born governess under his roof. What about the Thorpes? They'd take you in if I asked them to."

"Mrs. Thorpe treats me like a scullery maid, and Mr. Thorpe…well, he's your husband's closest friend, and considering how Mr. Hewitt feels about me…"

"Mm…There's Max Thurston. He adores you." The eccentric playwright had formed a warm friendship with Viola in recent months.

Shaking her head, Nell said, "It wouldn't look right, me living alone with a gentleman."

"Yes, but everyone knows that Max is, shall we say, immune to feminine temptations."

"Most people know that. It would still be scandalous. I *could* stay here, you know. It doesn't bother me to be alone, and it would only be for a little while." With any luck.

"Are you quite sure, my dear?"

Nell wasn't at all sure, but there didn't seem to be much of an option, so she said, with as much determination as she could muster, "Absolutely. I'll keep the doors locked and the curtains drawn. No one will even know I'm here."

CHAPTER THREE

*D*ON'T YOU EVER FORGET THERE *are eyes out there, watching your every move.*

Skinner's implicit threat echoed over and over in Nell's mind as she lay awake in her big bed that night on the third floor of Palazzo Hewitt, as Will had scornfully dubbed it. Despite her exhaustion, sleep eluded her. The heat was partly to blame. Though the windows on both sides of the corner room were wide open, it was a sweltering night, and the few breezes that wafted through the big room felt like gusts of heat from an opened oven door.

For the most part, though, Nell's restiveness was born of her sense of complete isolation. She felt exposed and forsaken in this huge mansion with it ghostly, sheet-draped furniture, regardless of the fact that she was there of her own volition.

Having never been in this house when it wasn't occupied by a swarm of family and servants, Nell hadn't counted on the utter, preternatural *emptiness* of it. There were no muffled voices reverberating through the walls, no opening and shutting of doors, no footsteps, no *life.* Just the faint, faraway ticking of the grandfather clock in the front parlor downstairs, which she'd never recalled hearing in her bedroom before, even in the middle of the night.

Rising out of bed, she crossed to the mantel clock, peering closely to make out the time in the thin moonlight: almost one in the morning. One would think that, having been awake for some twenty-two hours, after only five hours of sleep the night before, she'd be too exhausted to be sleepless, no matter how uneasy she felt.

Wanting to get her mane of sweat-dampened hair off her neck, Nell opened her top dresser drawer to search for the thin length of velvet she used to tie her hair back when she slept, because it resisted slipping off during the night. While rummaging among her little collection of gloves and collars and ribbons, she came upon a neatly folded, tissue-wrapped swath of silk tucked away in the back—the scarf Will Hewitt had been wearing the last time she saw him, back in January.

Nell had come to the railroad station on that blisteringly cold morning to see him off on his train to San Francisco, from whence he would board a steamer bound for Shanghai. It was to be a long and grueling journey, one destined to last perhaps years, one he hadn't been looking forward to, but felt compelled to embark on in order to put some distance between them.

Leaving Boston meant leaving not just her and Gracie, but his new position teaching forensic studies at Harvard medical school, which she knew he'd found rewarding. They'd never spoken frankly about his reasons for the trip, about the feelings that had arisen between them over the nearly three years of their acquaintance. Such feelings could lead nowhere, given her clandestine marriage. As a Catholic, divorce was a pointless option; she would be excommunicated should she ever remarry. For as long as she lived, Nell was destined to remain a spinster. And an intimate relationship outside of marriage, should it ever become known, would ruin her; she would lose her home with the Hewitts, her job, but worst of all, Gracie.

Will had understood this, which was why he'd chosen to take his extended sojourn away from Boston as a reprieve from the agony of their being together, yet ultimately apart. He'd been surprised to see her at the railroad station that morning, until she'd reminded him of the offer he'd made to her once, in a moment of weakness: one kiss from her—just one, he would never ask for another—and he would remain in Boston. They would go on as before, never speaking of those things better left unsaid. The kiss would be the end of it.

Ah, but the kiss, when it came, had been the end of nothing, and the promise of far too much. It had been wondrous, devastating, the admission of a secret longing that should never have been acknowledged. A door had been opened, and they both knew, without having to discuss it, that if they walked through that door, she could lose everything.

And so he'd boarded that train just as it was pulling out of the station, for her sake, his scarf flying off as he'd sprinted across the platform. Nell had picked it up off the granite pavement, her damp cheeks smarting in the cold, and brought it home. She'd taken his top hat, too, which had dropped to the ground during the kiss, and stored it in a hatbox on the top shelf of her clothespress.

Unwrapping the tissue for the first time since tucking the scarf away in the drawer, Nell rubbed the liquid-smooth silk between her fingers. She unfolded it and held it to her nose, inhaling a whisper of Bay Rum, a trace of tobacco. In the months before leaving Boston, Will had cut down dramatically on the number of cigarettes he smoked, but he'd had one that morning while waiting for his train. *Something to soothe me and keep me occupied when I can't quite abide the world and my role in it.*

The bittersweet scent of the scarf made Nell's eyes sting. God, how she'd missed him these past six months—that droll wit, that intimate smile, that velvety-deep voice, British-accented from his youthful exile in England. It was as if a great void had been carved from her chest, leaving her empty, needy. She'd always prided herself on her independence and self-reliance, yet here she was, close to tears over the absence of someone who could never be more to her than a friend—the dearest friend she'd ever had. How had this man—this cardsharp, this rake—come to feel like the other half of herself?

There came a muted creak from the hallway. Nell turned to see a yellowish ribbon of light beneath the door to her room; she'd left the hall lights off when she'd gone to bed.

Heart kicking, she shoved the scarf back in the drawer and plucked a hatpin from the porcelain holder on her dresser. A door squeaked open, the door from the hall to the adjacent nursery.

I could crack any lock in this house in less than a minute.

Nell crossed herself with a quaking hand, whispering a hurried prayer to St. Dismas. She padded on bare, silent feet to the hall door and stood, listening.

Through the next door down, which led to the nursery, she heard that one loose floorboard groan beneath the Persian rug. He must be looking for her. He'd notice the door connecting her room to the nursery and try that next.

Very cautiously, so as not to betray her presence, she opened the door to the hall and ran. As she passed the open nursery door, a man yelled, "Whoa there!"

Nell tore down the gaslit hallway, footsteps gaining from behind. She was almost at the landing when he seized her from behind, toppling her off balance.

She twisted faceup as she hit the carpeted floor, hauling back with the hatpin. *Go for an eye,* she thought as he fell on top of her.

"Nell!" He grabbed her wrist—grabbed both of her wrists—and pinned them to the floor, saying, "Bloody hell. Are you trying to blind me?"

She stared up at the familiar, darkly handsome face, a lock of inky hair hanging over his forehead.

"Will? Oh, my God." This was real, he was actually here, it was actually Will. Nell shook her head as if it would settle her whirling thoughts. "I'm...I'm sorry," she said on a flutter of nervous laughter. "I...I thought you were Skinner."

"Skinner? *Charlie* Skinner?" Will released her wrists and levered himself off her, pushing his hair back into place. "What the devil would he be doing here in the middle of the night?"

"What are *you* doing here?" she asked as she rose onto her elbows.

"I might ask you the same thing." Rising to his feet—awkwardly, given the old bullet wound in his leg—he offered her his hand. "Aren't you supposed to be on the Cape?"

"Something's come up," Nell said as she took his hand.

He helped her off the floor, his gaze lighting on her bare arms and legs. Heat flooded her face as she realized her state of undress; all she had on was her summer night shift, a short, sleeveless wisp of tissue-thin linen.

He gallantly turned his back, saying, "I, um...I'll fetch your wrapper."

She followed him on rubbery legs to her room, her arms wrapped rather pointlessly around herself, her mind a turmoil of embarrassment, joy, and confusion. Will's long-legged gait was perhaps a bit more graceful than it had been when she'd last seen him. She hoped he hadn't gone back to numbing his pain with opiates.

"Will, why *are* you here?" she asked as he lifted her blue plaid wrapper from the foot of her bed and handed it to her, all the while keeping his gaze discreetly averted. "I thought you'd still be in Shanghai."

"I came back a bit earlier than I'd expected," he said as he lit the candle on her nightstand. He turned as she was shrugging into the wrapper, crossed to her in one stride, and tugged it down off her shoulders.

She sucked in a breath. "What—?"

"How did this happen?" he asked, gripping her left arm just below the ring of bruises there. "These are finger-marks. Someone's been manhandling you."

"Skinner," she said on a sigh.

He met her gaze, eyes shadowed and jaw outthrust in that ominous scowl she'd found so intimidating when she was first getting to know him. He frowned at the bruises, stroking a thumb over them, the gentle friction raising goose bumps up and down her arm. "What happened?"

Nell sat on the edge of the bed, gathering the wrapper about her, and buttoned it from the throat down it while she told Will about Skinner's visit. Will leaned against the bedpost with his arms crossed as he listened, swearing under his breath from time to time.

Pushing off the bedpost, hands fisted, he said, "That cur needs to be taught a lesson."

"I'm more concerned with Detective Cook. I doubt Skinner even considered other suspects once he realized he could railroad Detective Cook. If it's left up to him, Cook will hang for sure. I've got to find out what really happened, how this Johnny Cassidy ended up dead."

"Ah, Nell…" Will raked his hands through his hair. "You and your missions of justice."

"Colin Cook is my friend, Will," Nell said with conviction. "He's a good man, and I'm not about to let him hang if there's anything I can do about it."

"Of course not," he said with a droll little smile. "You're not that kind of friend—well I know it. But you do realize that, by going up against Skinner, you're going up against the entire Boston Police Department. You'll get no aid from that quarter— quite the opposite. Constables stick together."

"I'm not saying it will be easy."

"Nothing with you ever is." Will lowered himself onto the bed, reclining on his side as casually as if they were any two chums having a late-night chat. That easy intimacy was something she'd missed terribly these past six months. "So, how is it that you propose to extract the good Detective Cook from Constable Skinner's talons?"

"It would help if I could find him, and then he could tell me what really happened."

"And why he's evading justice." After a thoughtful pause, Will said, "I, er, don't suppose you've seriously considered the possibility that he's guilty."

"Of murder?" She shook her head. "Impossible. I assume he fled because he knows it *looks* as if he did murder, and he doesn't want to hang for a crime he didn't commit."

"Watch those assumptions, Cornelia," Will said with a little wag of the finger. It was a familiar admonition.

"All right, then, perhaps his disappearance wasn't voluntary. Perhaps the real murderer had something to do with it." Nell leaned back onto the pillows mounded against her headboard, wrapping her arms around her updrawn legs. "There are a thousand questions that need answering. I don't even know the circumstances of the crime, who this Johnny Cassidy was, why they think Cook did it. I must find him. Perhaps his wife knows something."

"Do you know her?"

She shook her head. "We've never met, but Cook speaks of her often, in very loving terms. She's Irish, like him. He quit drinking when he married her. That's all I really know about her. I don't even know her first name. He always calls her Mrs. Cook."

"I don't suppose you've any idea where they live."

"He bought a new house after he was promoted to the state constabulary. He said it was on…" She plumbed her memory. "Something…something to do with the Revolutionary War. Lafayette? Is there a Lafayette Street in Boston?"

"There's a Fayette Street," Will said. "It's in the Church Street District. Nice little neighborhood south of the Public Gardens."

"That must be it," Nell said. "I'll go there tomorrow and find the house, introduce myself to Mrs. Cook, see if she knows anything. Then I'll head up to the North End and poke about a bit."

"Poke about a bit." Will flopped down on his back, rubbing his hands over his face. "In the North End." He emitted a sound that was somewhere between a groan and a chuckle. "Nell, Nell, Nell..."

"That *is* where this killing took place," she pointed out.

"That is where a great many killings take place, my dear Cornelia. And a great many beatings and knifings and thefts and rapes, as you must no doubt be well aware."

"I know all about the North End, Will."

"Oh, you do, do you?" Raising himself up on an elbow, he looked her in the eye and said, "How much time have you actually spent up there, Nell?"

"I'm there almost every Sunday morning."

"In the tame, rosy blush of dawn, with Brady escorting you to and from church in the family brougham. I think it's safe to say you've never spent any appreciable time there. If you did, you'd know it's not a place for a prim little thing like you to be 'poking about.' It's where the worst gutter-prowlers and roughnecks in Boston live and prey on each other."

"I've been in bad neighborhoods before, Will," she reminded him. "I've associated with those gutter-prowlers and roughnecks. Don't forget, I was a dipping-girl myself once."

"Having your pocket picked is the least of the threats you'll encounter up there." He looked away for a moment with a preoccupied frown, as if sorting something out in his head. "If you insist on doing this, I'm going with you."

"I'll probably end up protecting *you*," she said with a grin. "It's an Irish neighborhood, you know. I'm one of them."

"At one time, perhaps. Not anymore. You look like a Brahmin and talk like a Brahmin and act like a Brahmin. You'd be mad to wander 'round there unescorted. And as for your staying here all alone…" He shook his head as he sat up, stretching his back. "It's far too risky. I've no doubt Skinner *could* pick these door locks fairly easily. That's how *I* got in. What if I'd been he?"

"I would have stuck him in the eye with my hatpin," Nell said.

"Whereupon he might very well have bludgeoned you with his truncheon."

"He probably would have just shot me," Nell said.

"Shot you? They let that mullethead carry a sidearm?"

"All the constables seem to be carrying them lately."

"You realize half of them started out as battlers and sneak thieves themselves. They didn't have what it took to be successful crooks, so they joined the police force. Bad enough they've been given uniforms and badges—now they've been armed, as well?" Will shook his head disgustedly. "You've got to come stay at my house."

"*What?*"

"You'll be safe there."

"Will, you know I can't do that. What would your house-keeper think? And your neighbors?"

With a rueful smile, he said, "Have I ever let the opinions of others rule my actions?"

"No, but I have. I must. You know that, Will. I'd be ruined if I were to be seen coming and going from your house at all hours."

"Yes, but—"

"Will, why *did* you come back so soon?" she asked, wanting to redirect the conversation. "You never really answered that."

He levered himself off the bed to stroll around the room, looking about curiously in the semidarkness. "These are quite nice," he said as he perused the new drawings she'd tacked up on the wall. "This sketch of Gracie, in particular. You really captured that spark in her eye."

"Thank you," Nell said, wondering why he was so reticent to discuss his reasons for returning from Shanghai. "She's beginning to ask rather awkward questions."

"That's what children do."

"Questions about her parentage. She's overhearing things, things that are going to start adding up for her fairly soon."

"Such as?"

"Such as who fathered her."

Will stood looking at the sketch in silence.

Nell said, "I can't keep putting her off forever, Will. Sooner or later, she'll find out, and I think it would be best if she found out from you."

"We've had this conversation before, Nell. I'm not the kind of man any young girl would want to acknowledge as her father."

"She already views you as a father figure. She still insists she wants to live with us after we're married."

With a sigh, Will continued his pensive tour of her room. Pausing in front of her dresser, he pulled the gray silk scarf from the open drawer. "Is this mine?"

She hesitated, her cheeks warming. "Yes, it's...the one you were wearing at the train station when you left. It fell off. I've been keeping it for you. Your hat, too."

He stood looking at the scarf, seemingly lost in thought. After a long moment, he said, "Shanghai hasn't changed. Still murky and mysterious and steeped in sin. Just as seductive as ever, in its own perverse way—if one is susceptible to that sort of thing."

She had to ask: "Did you smoke opium?"

He took so long answering that she wondered if he'd heard her. Finally he said, "Yes."

CHAPTER FOUR

“O H, WILL.”

“Just once,” he said over his shoulder. “I, um, I’d
drunk more than usual at the card table one night—
I’d been feeling lonely—so of course I got careless and started
losing. I cashed in and just…wandered the alleyways, smoking
cigarettes, thinking too much, missing…”

He rubbed the back of his neck, looked at her, then away. “I
followed a whiff of opium smoke into this squalid little room.
I woke up there the next morning with a smoking pistol in my
hand, sick with shame. It had taken so much effort, so much pain
and sickness to get myself free of that poison. I thought about you,
and how appalled you would be, how disgusted.”

“I would have understood,” she said.

“Because you understand my weaknesses.” Turning to face
her, he said, “You’ve never had any illusions about me. Why would
you, considering the shape I was in when you met me? You know
how flawed I am, yet still you’ve put up with me.”

“I don’t just put up with you, Will,” she said quietly. “You know that.”

Will met her eyes, and she knew he was remembering those
final moments under the eave of the railroad station—the tears,
the anguished parting…the breath-stealing kiss.

Just one, he’d implored. *I won’t ask for a second. Ever. I promise.
And I’ll remain in Boston, and we can go on as before.*

He looked down at the scarf, absently running it through his
hands. “I went directly from the hop joint to the Pacific Mail
Steamship Company and booked passage back to San Francisco.
I…actually thought about staying there.”

"In San Francisco?"

"It's gone through some remarkable changes in the past few years. It's becoming a real city, yet still with a certain raw western flavor that appeals to me. And I'd won a house on Sacramento Street in a game of faro—quite a nice one, actually, about half again as big as my house here, and newly built. I won it from a real estate speculator, and he could well afford to lose it, believe me—he's making money hand over fist in that town. I thought about staying and…losing myself, you know? Let this brand new city just grow up around me like a giant cocoon. Forget who I'd been before, where I'd been before, forget…" He looked away from Nell's gaze, his jaw tight. "In the end, I got on that train."

"How long have you been back?" she asked.

"Since yesterday evening."

Steeling herself, she asked, "Will you be…leaving again, or…?"

He shook his head, his gaze on the floor, hands shoved in his trouser pockets. "I don't know, Nell. I really don't. I had lunch with Isaac Foster today, and he said I'd be welcome back at Harvard any time. He's keeping the position open for me, because there's no one else who's qualified to teach forensic studies. He even offered me a full professorship, but with a catch—I've got to give him a five-year commitment."

"Ah. Well, you can hardly blame him, can you?"

With a rueful smile, Will said, "He knows me all too well." Sobering a bit, he said, "I've received another offer, as well—or rather, a request. From the president."

"The president." He couldn't mean…

"There was a letter from the White House on top of the stack of mail that was waiting for me when I got home yesterday. President Grant sent it a couple of weeks ago."

"Wait. Does he know you? I know he knows *of* you." During the war, Ulysses Grant, then General-in-Chief of the Union forces, had been quoted as declaring Will the finest battle surgeon in the Army.

"Our paths crossed a few times during the war," Will said. "The last time was right before I was captured by the Rebs. In his letter, Grant said he toasted my memory with some 'damned fine whiskey' when my name showed up on the Andersonville death roll. Of course, he thought I was dead for years after that, just like everyone else."

"Because that was what you wanted people to think," Nell reminded him.

"Yes, well, in any event," Will continued, "as Grant explained it, he and his advisers have been concerned of late about the escalating tensions between France and Prussia."

"That business about the Emperor Napoleon not wanting King Wilhelm's cousin to assume the throne of Spain?"

"You've been reading the papers, I see. It's actually a bit more complicated than that, yet at the same time rather primitive. Napoleon and Wilhelm have been snapping at each other for years like a couple of dogs staking out their territories. They're itching for a fight, both of them. It's only a matter of time—at this point, days or weeks—before they launch themselves into a full-fledged war."

"Don't tell me Grant wants us to become involved."

"Good Lord, no. He's assured me we'll be neutral, as will England. The thing is, our ambassador to France, Elihu Washburne, is a hometown friend of Grant's, and a very powerful man to whom Grant owes his career, both in the military and in politics. Washburne's sympathies are very much with France, and he's determined to remain in Paris, come what may, never mind that city's been a powder keg of late even without the threat of war. Washburne has asked Grant to send him various support personnel in case things get ugly, including the best field surgeon he could muster up."

Nell expelled a lungful of air, not liking where this was headed. "The president realizes you're among the living, then?"

"He found out when he asked the deans of the Harvard and Columbia medical schools whom they would recommend, and they both mentioned me."

"I'm impressed."

"Don't be. It's just serendipity. I'd written an article on the nature of bullet wounds for the *Boston Medical and Surgical Journal* shortly before I left for Shanghai, and it was published in May. The article dealt with certain conclusions I'd drawn based upon my experience in field surgery during the war. Both deans happened to recall me from my service with the Army. When Grant asked for candidates, I was fresh in their memory."

"So you're weighing two options now," she said. "Harvard or France."

"Grant has asked for my answer by the beginning of next week, so that he can find someone else if I decline."

"And what about Harvard? When does Isaac want his answer?"

"He has no particular deadline. He said if I'm not ready to accept his offer this year, he hopes I'll do so next year, or the year after. He just wants me on board."

"How is Isaac? I haven't seen him in a few weeks."

"I know. He said he was sorry he and Emily hadn't gotten to spend more time with you before you left for the Cape. That's where he thinks you are right now. When I told him I was going to look for you and Gracie in the park this afternoon, he told me you'd left this morning. To say I was disappointed would be a grotesque understatement. He suggested I head down to the Cape myself, but of course that was out of the question. I couldn't imagine sharing a roof with my old man for any length of time."

"You could always stay in the boathouse, as you did when you were younger."

"How did you know that?"

"Your mother told me once. She said you loved the lapping of the water."

"I loved the distance from her and my father. I could bear *her* now, of course, but not him. That's hopeless. And as for Harry..." Will shook his head. "I hate to think of my own brother as irredeemable, but the more time passes, the clearer it becomes that he's selfish and depraved and destined to remain so. Perhaps if he hadn't brutalized you as he did, I'd feel differently. As it is, I fear there's no hope for him."

"Harry probably won't be coming to the Cape. He didn't last year, either, in protest over your parents' insistence upon keeping me in their employ. Then, again, if the little woman gets her way..."

"The little woman? It's a fait accompli, then?"

"He and Cecilia were joined in matrimony April second," Nell said with a smile that felt just shy of a smirk. "Your mother said the Pratts threw the hugest, most lavish bridal dinner she'd ever attended, never mind it was Lent. She said Cecilia was festooned with jewels, some of which were said to have been gifts from various former beaus and fiancés."

With a wry little chuckle, Will said, "Almost makes me feel sorry for Harry. He has no idea what he's gotten himself into, shackling himself to that cold-eyed, avaricious little nit."

"They've been honeymooning in Europe, but they're due to return next month, and I understand Cecilia wants to visit Falconwood after they get back."

"What Cecilia wants, Cecilia gets. I don't envy you, having to put up with the two of them—although Martin is there, isn't he? I expect his presence will have a chastening effect on Harry." Twenty-three-year-old Martin, the youngest of the Hewitts' three living sons, was the only member of his family with whom Will remained on genuinely affectionate terms.

"Martin isn't there yet," Nell said. "He's to deliver a sermon at King's Chapel this Sunday, and then he can go, but he'll have to come back early next month to formally begin his ministerial duties. He was ordained there last month as an assistant pastor."

"He was ordained in a Unitarian church?" Will said laughingly. "Saint August must have been apoplectic."

"He refused to attend the ordination ceremony. Your father called him a heretic, told him he was jeopardizing his immortal soul."

"You're joking."

"I'd never seen him like that. Martin was utterly serene, of course. He said he was sorry your father found it so upsetting, but that it was a well thought out decision, and he was very content with it. That was about a month and a half ago. He's been sharing digs since then with a friend at one of the Harvard dormitories while he looks for a place of his own. He says it's a bit cramped, the two of them in one room, but that it's been a 'refreshingly humbling experience,' given the privilege he grew up with."

"Martin will make a good minister," Will said with a smile. "He's a positive thinker, and a born diplomatist. So, I take it Nurse Parrish is looking after Gracie until you can join them on the Cape, or has Eileen pretty much taken over that end of things?"

"Oh." Nell wished she didn't have to convey this particular piece of news. "I'm sorry, Will. Nurse Parrish…"

She didn't have to finish the sentence. Will seemed to deflate. "Damn," he whispered.

The elderly Edna Parrish, who'd served as nanny not only to Will and his brothers, but to their mother as well, had long been regarded by the Hewitts as a member of the family.

"When?" Will asked.

"March. It happened during a Sunday service. Your mother was sitting on one side of her, I on the other, and we caught her as she slumped over. By the time we got her stretched out on the pew, she was gone. I tried to revive her, but it was no use. It was her heart, I think. It just gave out."

"I don't understand. You were in church with her and my mother? At *King's Chapel?*"

"I, um…it was decided that Gracie should start attending services with your mother. She needed someone along to look after her in church, and given your mother's infirmity and Nurse Parrish's age…" Nell shrugged.

"Yes, but you're a Catholic. It seems rather an unreasonable requirement on the part of my mother, I'd say."

"She didn't require it," Nell said. "She didn't even suggest it. I did."

"You *volunteered* to attend Protestant services? *You?*"

Will's surprise was understandable. More than once, she and Will had argued over her unwavering devotion to the demands of her faith, particularly as regarded her refusal to divorce Duncan. He found it unfathomable that she would choose to remain married to a man she didn't love, an imprisoned felon who'd brutalized her, no less. She'd tried to explain it to him, to make him understand how the Catholicism she'd embraced when she was at her lowest had helped her to remake herself. He maintained that her rigid adherence to Church law had become, in recent years, a crutch that she no longer needed.

I want what's best for you, he'd told her last autumn, *and what's best is to divorce Duncan. Then, if you ever choose to remarry, and you are* excommunicated, *it will be the* Church *turning its back on you, not God.*

That little speech had affected Nell more profoundly than Will could possibly have foreseen. She'd reiterated it countless times in her mind these past months, pondering its repercussions, its consequences. It was no simple thing for her to dismiss the faith of her fathers, the faith that had been her bulwark for so many years; yet neither could she dismiss Will's simple logic, his heartfelt plea.

It was a plea with an unspoken implication. Were she free of the restrictions of the Church, she could be free of Duncan, free to be courted by another man. Of course, Will had never disclosed any feelings for her that ran deeper than heartfelt friendship—not in words. He wouldn't have, knowing that she was fated to remain a married woman, and therefore wasn't free to hear such a declaration.

Then had come the kiss, after which they were to go on as before. It had been his explicit promise, and Nell knew he would try to keep it. That kiss would never be mentioned again, unless Nell were to bring it up. Even at Will Hewitt's most dissipated, he'd always had the instincts of a gentleman.

"So, do you still attend Catholic services?" Will asked.

Nell nodded. "Early mass at St. Stephen's every Sunday." Or rather, most Sundays; she'd actually skipped one or two recently, a first for her.

"Two church services in a row every Sunday," Will said with a little shudder. "That's positively heroic."

With a roll of the eyes, Nell said, "You still haven't told me why you broke in here in the middle of the night. What were you doing in the nursery?"

"I brought Gracie a gift from Shanghai, a set of miniature Chinese furniture for her dollhouse. I…brought you something, too. I was going to leave it here for you to find when you got back from the Cape. I dropped it when I saw you running down the hall."

Will crossed into the nursery through the door connecting the two rooms, returning a moment later with a long, paper-wrapped tubular object in one hand and his hat in the other. He retrieved a little folding knife from inside his coat—a scalpel, she saw.

"I was going to hang this on the wall," he said as he cut the twine securing the rough brown paper. "My intent is to have it properly framed under glass, to protect it. It's a couple of hundred years old."

He peeled away the paper and unrolled a silken scroll about three feet wide and six or seven feet long.

"Oh, Will," Nell breathed as he laid it across the bed so that she could get a good look at it. It was a painting executed in watercolor and gold leaf of a beautiful, smiling woman in a lavish headdress and Chinese robes, standing on a lotus surrounded by clouds and waves. "It's exquisite."

Sitting at the foot of the bed, Will said, "It's the Guanyin Buddha. She's a bodhisattva. That's someone who's attained a high level of enlightenment, but who postpones paradise in order to help others. She reminded me so much of you that I knew you had to have this."

The woman in the painting had raven hair and delicate, Oriental features. "I can't say there's much of a resemblance," Nell said.

"The Guanyin is the goddess of mercy and compassion," he said. "She exists to free others from their suffering and help them overcome their obstacles. I'd say there's a very strong resemblance."

Nell looked up to find Will regarding her in that quietly intent way of his. The candlelight softened his sharply carved, world-weary features—the shadowed eyes and hard jaw—making him look younger than his thirty-five years. There was a suggestion of something in his eyes, a vulnerability, a quiet yearning.

"If it weren't for you," he said quietly, "I would have long since succumbed to my demons. I'd have died at the end of a noose, or with a needle in my arm. You drained the poison from me. You turned me back into some semblance of the man I was before... the war, and all that. I owe you more than I could possibly repay. You must know that."

"You don't owe me anything, Will."

"Regardless, it would ill repay you for all your kindness to allow you to remain here alone and vulnerable. I'm going to stay here with you. I'll sleep next door, in the nursery."

"What?" She got off the bed and crossed to him, frowning in bewilderment. "But, Will…"

"It isn't safe, you staying here alone."

"Will, you just said you were concerned about my reputation. If that's the case, how could you even think about sharing this house with me?"

"No one will know. I'll use the back entrance. The windows are all curtained. I won't be seen."

"But…what if someone *does* see you? What if—?"

"What if Skinner finds out you're here and breaks in some night to teach you a lesson?" He closed his hands over her shoulders and ducked his head toward hers, gentling his voice. "Look, Nell, I understand why you're staying behind to help Cook. I admire your loyalty to your friends and your willingness to stick your neck out, I always have. But I can't and won't let you make a sitting duck of yourself. Make no mistake. I'm not asking if I can stay here. I'm telling you."

"When did you become so…so *damned* dictatorial?"

"And when did you start cursing like a sailor?" he asked with a chuckle. "Not that I don't approve. I do—heartily. Your lofty character has always been a bit too overplayed for my taste."

"It's good to see you laugh," Nell said. "I've missed you, Will. I'm…" She swallowed to ease the tightness in her throat. "I'm glad you're back."

Will nodded, his smile fading. He leaned down to kiss the top of her head. "Good night, Nell," he said, and retired to the nursery.

CHAPTER FIVE

"**W**HAT A CHARMING AREA," NELL said as Will knocked on the front door of the three-story red-brick townhouse to which the Cooks' Fayette Street neighbors had directed them. Through the lace-swagged, glass-paned door could be seen a small entrance hall with a curved stairway, and beyond it, a corridor terminating in a pair of glass doors. "Reminds me of Beacon Hill."

Will said, "That's because most of these houses were built by the same carpenters and masons, for their own families."

Shielding her eyes against the late morning sun to peer up at the house, Nell said, "Cook must be making good money as a state constable, to be able to afford a place like this."

"Cops have ways of supplementing their incomes," Will said dryly.

"I doubt he's taking payoffs," Nell said. "I know he did at one time, on a small scale, but after the hearings and all that, I would imagine he's toeing the line. I know *I* would."

"You're the type who learns from the past. Most people can't be bothered to examine their own lives or question their actions. They operate more on dumb instinct than self-reflection."

"Feeling a bit more pedantic than usual this morning?"

Nell had expected some flippant reply to match her teasing tone—*Cheeky vixen*, something of that nature. Instead, Will merely said, "I suppose."

It had felt strange, last night, sleeping so near to Will, their beds aligned headboard to headboard on either side of the wall separating her bedroom from the nursery. He'd insisted on leaving the connecting door open during the night, reasoning that he could hardly protect her if he couldn't hear the sounds of an intruder in her room. She'd lain awake for some time, listening to the restless creaks of Gracie's bed and wondering if the situation felt as oddly intimate to him as it did to her.

She awoke this morning to the sound of her name on Will's lips. Squinting against a searing haze of morning sunlight, she saw him standing at the foot of her bed. He was in his shirt-sleeves, and leaning against the bedpost with his arms crossed. How long had he been there, she wondered, watching her sleep.

"My word," she'd muttered groggily when she managed to focus on the mantel clock. "Is it really almost nine o'clock?" She couldn't remember the last time she'd slept so late.

"I've got coffee on," he said as he turned and crossed to the door, "and it's not half bad. It's the one thing I know how to do in a kitchen. But it'll burn if it sits on the stove much longer, so don't tarry."

Just as Will lifted his hand to knock again on the Cooks' front door, there came a flicker of movement from within the house. The doors at the far end of the corridor opened and a petite, dark-haired woman walked toward them. She wore a brown paisley frock and a bib apron, with a wide-brimmed straw hat clutched in front of her like a shield. As she got closer, Nell saw that she was little older than herself, thirty at most.

The young woman cracked the door open just enough to peer out warily at Nell and Will. Her eyes, Nell saw, were puffy, her nose shiny-red; nevertheless, she was strikingly pretty, with creamy skin and dainty features. "Yes?"

"We're here to see Mrs. Cook," Will said, reaching into his coat for his calling card.

In a rusty-damp voice inflected with a subtle Irish brogue, she said, "I'm Chloe Cook."

"Ah." Will handed her his card, saying, "I'm Dr. Hewitt, and this is Miss Sweeney. I know this is a difficult time for you, Mrs. Cook, but I wonder if we might impose upon you for a—"

"Sweeney?" Chloe Cook looked up from the card to meet Nell's gaze. "Would you be *Nell* Sweeney, then?"

"That's right," Nell said. "Your husband has mentioned me, I take it."

"Yes, of course, of course. Do come in," Chloe said, opening the door wider and gesturing them inside. "It's so good to meet you at last, Miss Sweeney, even if...well, even under these..." Her chin quivered; she pulled a handkerchief from her apron pocket.

Nell said, "I truly *am* sorry to disturb you at such a time, Mrs. Cook. We...we're here because...well, we thought perhaps we might be of some help in sorting through—"

"They think he—" A sob rose in Chloe's throat. She pressed the handkerchief to her mouth. "They think...they think..."

"I know." Nell said soothingly.

"He's in terrible trouble."

"I know. We know."

"I've been trying to be strong for Colin's sake," Chloe managed as she wiped her face, "but it's just...it's so hard. I don't know what to do. I'm...I'm so bewildered."

"So are we," Will said. "But we want to help. We find it difficult to believe that he did what they're saying he did. That's why we're here. Perhaps there's someplace we can talk?"

"Yes, of course. Um, yes. Please." Turning, Chloe ushered them down the corridor, which smelled of fresh paint, and through the open glass doors, which led to a sunny little garden out back. "W-would you like some tea, or..."

"No, really," Nell said. "We don't want to impose."

"It's already made," Chloe said, indicating a porcelain teapot sitting on an iron table next to a half-empty cup. "Make yourselves at home—please. I'll be right back." She turned and disappeared into the house.

"She's so young," Nell whispered to Will as he held a chair out for her. "Somehow I thought she'd be older."

"Cook is about forty, I would think," Will said as he seated himself. "There'd be about a ten or twelve year difference in their ages, not so much. Do you know how long they've been married?"

Nell shook her head. "He's never talked very much about his personal life."

"Hopefully his wife will be more forthcoming. She's very well spoken, don't you think?"

In an exaggerated Irish brogue, Nell asked, "More so than most of us ignorant paddywhacks, d'ye mean?"

Casting a baleful look in her direction, Will said, "I mean she sounds like someone with a good upbringing, perhaps even an education. That *is* rare among Irish immigrants, as you're very well aware. Just makes me curious, that's all."

Chloe returned carrying a tray laden with two cups, a sugar bowl, a creamer, and a plate of prettily molded cookies. "These are from yesterday, but they're still good." She set the tray on the table, untied her apron, and draped it over the empty fourth chair. It was only then that Nell noticed the styling of Chloe's frock, a loose, wrapper-like garment with a wide double panel down the front secured with frogs over the young woman's rounded belly.

Observing the direction of Nell's gaze, Chloe rested a hand on her stomach and said, with a watery little smile, "Colin and I are expecting a blessed event in October. Our first."

"Oh. I...I didn't realize," Nell said. "That's...that's wonderful."

"Congratulations," Will said.

Chloe glanced up at Nell as she poured the tea. "You're wondering why he didn't tell you."

"Well..."

Setting the cups in front of her guests, Chloe said, "It's not the first time I've been in the family way. We've lost three wee ones, Colin and I. Our first was stillborn, a little boy we named Patrick, and the other two never even made it this far."

"I'm so sorry," Nell said. "That must be incredibly painful." It was a pain Nell knew all too well, having suffered, after Duncan's final, savage beating, a miscarriage that had more than likely left her sterile.

"I trust you're seeing a physician," said Will as he pulled Chloe's chair out for her.

"Yes, indeed, Dr. Mathers."

"I know of him," Will said. "He's very well thought of."

"He's given me a list of rules meant to keep this babe tight in the womb. No strenuous activity—I can't even weed this disastrous garden. No...restrictive garments."

"Good for Mathers," Will said. "Whenever I see a pregnant woman in a corset, I want to throttle her."

"Dr. Hewitt is a physician," Nell said, by way of explaining his frankness.

"Non-practicing," he said. "My only experience with expectant mothers was during medical school at Edinburgh, back before the war."

"Is it true," Chloe asked, "what Dr. Mathers says, that there's no way to stop a...mishap, if you feel one coming on? He...he said it was God's will, that all I could do is lie down and 'let nature take its course,' but he's so old, you know. You're younger. You were trained so recently. Is there something new? Some tonic, or...?"

With an apologetic little shrug, Will said, "Bed rest is what we were taught to prescribe. Miss Sweeney actually has a good deal more experience with such matters than I do."

"I served as nurse to a doctor on Cape Cod for four years," Nell explained. "There are some herbs native to this country that the Indians use for that purpose, but no tonic per se. The best thing you can do is to try to prevent such a mishap by not over-exerting yourself."

"Oh, I've been pretty much staying at home," Chloe said, "reading, doing embroidery and watercolors…I'm bored out of my wits, but I don't mind. I don't mind looking this way, I don't mind any of it. I want this baby so badly—Colin, too. He hired a girl to come in at noon for the cooking and cleaning. I asked him not to tell people I'm expecting. He thinks I'm being superstitious, but that's really not it. There's just so much pity I can bear, and if…if anything were to happen to this baby…"

"Surely you've told your family," Nell said as she stirred sugar and milk into her tea.

"My parents are gone. I've just got the one older brother, James—he lives in New York. He's a constable, too. Colin has no kin at all in the States. He came over alone. I have a friend, Lily Booth, who lives around the corner. She's the only person I've told. She spent most of yesterday with me, trying to keep me calm for the sake of the baby."

"She was right to do so," Will said. "Given your condition, and your past history, it's best that you not allow yourself to become too overwrought."

"Your advice is well taken, Doctor," Chloe said, "but given what's happened…" She sat back wearily. "What they're saying Colin did…"

"We actually know very little about the circumstances," Nell said. "Detective Skinner paid a call on me yesterday afternoon, but he didn't tell me much."

Chloe grimaced. "He came to see me, too. Loathsome man. Colin can't bear him."

"All we know," Nell said, "is that Detective Cook is supposed to have shot someone named Johnny Cassidy at a place called Nabby's Inferno Tuesday night."

"When did you last see your husband?" Will asked Chloe.

"Tuesday afternoon. He came home for lunch. It's the one meal we always share together, because he sometimes works so late. He's often not home till after I've gone to sleep. I woke up yesterday morning and reached over to his side of the bed, but he wasn't there. The covers were undisturbed, and it was obvious his head had never lain on the pillow. I knew immediately that something was wrong."

"Did he happen to mention what he would be doing later on Tuesday?" Will asked. "Where he might be headed?"

"Colin doesn't talk much about his work, not the day-to-day specifics of it, but I do know that he spends most of his time in the North End. Fort Hill sometimes, and other areas, but mostly the North End. It's his job to deal with vice, and that's where the worst of it is. And it's only the worst of it that he troubles himself over, not the routine things—drunken sailors, pickpockets, street girls. It's the beat cops and watchmen who keep them in line, or try to. Colin goes after bigger game—gangs of thugs, slashers, rapists..."

"Dangerous work," Will said.

"I fret about him constantly." Chloe closed her eyes and shook her head. "Constantly. I wish to God he hadn't gone to work for the state constables. He didn't really want to. After that awful business in February, the hearings and all that..." Chloe's gaze lit on something over Nell's shoulder; she smiled. "Maureen. You're early today."

Nell and Will turned to find a moon-faced young woman in an apron and head rag unlatching the garden gate, a market basket over one arm. Eyeing Nell and Will with a kind of dull curiosity, she said, "They stayin' fer lunch?"

"Oh. Um..." Turning to Nell and Will, Chloe said, "That would be lovely, actually."

"Thank you all the same," Nell said, "but we can't stay. We've a great deal to accomplish this afternoon."

"Just you, then, missus?" Maureen asked.

"No, set two places," Chloe told her. "Out here, if you don't mind."

"Two?" Maureen stopped walking. "He ain't back, is he? Detective Cook?"

"No. No, he, er, he's not back. Mrs. Booth will be joining me for lunch."

Maureen nodded and entered the house through the back door.

Chloe sighed. "I'm not used to having help, but I don't think I like it very much. Or perhaps it's just…I don't know. I just never know what that girl is thinking."

"You'd mentioned the hearings in February," Nell prompted.

"Oh, those blasted hearings."

"Constable Skinner claims that there were secret sessions at which your husband testified," Nell said. "They seem to have made him even more of a pariah among his colleagues than he'd been before. I don't suppose you'd know anything about that."

"No, all Colin would tell me about the hearings was that he wasn't in any trouble and everything would turn out all right. It was his way of keeping me from worrying, but it had the opposite effect. I kept imagining the worst possible outcomes."

"Does your husband have any enemies?" Will asked. "Aside from Skinner. Someone who might want to see him hang for a murder he didn't commit?"

"Just Skinner's colleagues, the other city detectives. I can't think of anyone else."

"What about friends?" Nell asked. "Someone at City Hall, perhaps, who could tell us what really went on in those secret hearing sessions."

"Or who might have been privy to his dealings in the North End," Will added.

"Well, there's Ben Shute," Chloe said. "Ebenezer, really, but Colin calls him Ben. He's Superintendent of Pawnbrokers. A few years younger than Colin, mid-thirties, I should think—a bachelor. Lost an eye and a leg at Fredericksburg, poor fellow. Colin got to know him when he joined the Detectives' Bureau in City Hall. Their offices were on the same corridor."

"Are they just casual acquaintances," Will asked, "or...?"

"Oh, Ben is Colin's closest friend in the world, has been for years. I was surprised at first when the two of them hit it off so well. Ben is from a family of Maryland tobacco planters, very wealthy and well-connected. He's worth a fortune, but you'd never guess it."

To Nell, Will said, "We can stop at City Hall on our way back from Mass General and see if Mr. Shute will speak to us."

"It might help," Nell told Chloe, "if you could write us a brief letter of introduction so that Mr. Shute knows he can speak to us in confidence."

"Of course." Shaking her head, Chloe said, "I just wish Colin had taken Ben's advice and set himself up as a private detective when the bureau was disbanded. Ben said he'd recommend Colin to friends—you know, send business his way. There wouldn't have been much money in it, not at first, anyway, but he would have been his own man, answering only to himself. Colin really took to the idea—me, too."

"Why didn't he do it, then?" Nell asked.

"It was Major Jones, the fellow who's in charge of the state constabulary. He offered Colin a position, told him he was just the type of solid, upright man they needed. Colin turned it down. Jones increased the salary by quite a bit. Colin was fixing to turn it down again, but then we found out I was expecting. He said he wanted to give us the kind of life we deserved, the baby and me. We had a nice little house a few blocks away, in the South End, but he didn't think it was big enough anymore. I told him we could make do, but he said didn't want his child to grow up just making do, as he had. He wanted us to have nice furniture and clothes, a shiny new carriage, playthings for the baby. I've never cared about all that. I just wanted *him*. I wanted him safe. And now—" Her voice cracked; she looked away.

"Mrs. Cook." Nell leaned across the table to touch Chloe's arm. "I'm sorry this is so difficult, truly I am. But the more we can find out—"

"It's fine," Chloe said as she raised her teacup. "I'm fine. I'm very grateful to you for wanting to help. God knows what will happen to Colin if his fate is left in the hands of Constable Skinner." Smiling at Nell, she said, "Colin thinks very highly of you, you know, says you've got a whipcrack mind, and a certain way with people, with making them open up to you."

"She does, indeed," Will said, with a fleeting smile in Nell's direction. "Mrs. Cook, I must ask you this, and I beg you to be completely truthful and candid for your husband's sake. Have you had any contact with him at all since Tuesday? A note, perhaps—anything?"

"You can tell us in complete confidence," Nell assured her. "We would never—"

"If I knew where he was," Chloe said, "I wouldn't be half as wrought up about all this. He just…never came home. It's so unlike him to do something like that with no word to me. We haven't been apart this long since we were married."

"When was that?" Nell asked.

"The twenty-ninth of October, eighteen sixty-four. Colin had mustered out of the Army in September. We were married as soon as he was sure the police department would take him back."

"I take it you'd known him before the war, then," Nell said.

"Um, yes. Yes. Not well, but...I, er, wrote to him when I found out he'd enlisted. He wrote back. We established a correspondence that became...more affectionate, shall I say, than we had anticipated. It was in his final letter to me that he asked me to marry him, because he didn't know if he'd have the nerve to do it in person. Of course I accepted. Colin was..." Chloe gazed off in the direction of the overgrown, weed-choked garden. "He was unlike any man I'd ever known. So big, you know, with that commanding way about him, and those rough edges, but his heart..." She pressed her fist to her chest, her eyes shimmering. "It was his heart I got to know through the letters. It was his heart I fell in love with."

"Do you mind if I ask why you initiated this correspondence?" Will asked.

She turned to look at him.

He said, "You said you hadn't known him that long. It just seems a rather...bold gesture for a lady such as yourself. I'm curious as to what inspired it."

She hesitated, as if formulating her response. "I'd written to thank him for something."

"May I ask for what?"

"It's not important," Chloe said as she wiped up a drop of tea off the table with her napkin. "I mean, so far as all the rest of it goes. It has nothing to do with what happened. It couldn't have."

Will said, "I'm just asking because we really know so little about Detective Cook, and the more we can piece together about his background as a constable, the more information we'll have with which to—"

"It had nothing to do with his being a constable." Chloe said. "It was...something that happened before he joined the department.

"When *did* he join it?" Will asked.

"January of eighteen-sixty. He took a three-year leave to serve with the First Company Sharpshooters in September of 'sixty-one, but then he went back to the police afterwards."

"The Sharpshooters?" Will said. "I'm impressed."

With a spark of pride in her eyes, Chloe said, "They'd held recruiting trials for the Sharpshooters that summer. He had to hit a ten-inch target from two-hundred yards. He got ten bulls-eyes."

"Where did he learn to shoot like that?" Nell asked.

"In the old country," Chloe said. "He'd been part of Daniel O'Connell's Young Ireland movement to repeal the Act of Union and end discrimination against the Catholics. It was a fairly peaceful process till the famine, and then some of them had enough and took up arms. You know about the revolt in 'forty-eight, I assume."

"Of course," Nell said. "I was little at the time, and living over here, but my father and his mates could talk of nothing else."

"Colin was involved in that," Chloe said. "He was eighteen, and something of a hot-head, very passionate about the cause. The leadership wasn't what it could have been, though, and they failed miserably. Most of them were rounded up and transported to Van Diemen's Land—Tasmania, they call it now. Colin and some of the others escaped to America before they could arrest him."

"What did he do before he joined the police?" Nell asked.

"He mined coal in Pennsylvania for a few years. He came from a family of zinc miners in Tipperary, so it was familiar work to him. Of course, it was it backbreaking work, the conditions were appalling. The owners didn't give a fip how many of them got sick or died, so long as the profits kept coming. Colin joined a group of men who were trying to organize the miners, but they were almost as selfish and corrupt as the owners—not Colin, of course, but the others—so it came to nothing."

"That must have been discouraging for him," Will said, "especially after his experience in Ireland."

"Colin likes to say that good intentions are no match for a little power. Eventually he got fed up and made his way back to Boston."

"That would have been...some time in the 'fifties?" Nell asked.

Chloe nodded, raising her empty cup to her mouth. "Fifty-five, I believe. It was before we met."

"What did he do here?" Will asked. "How did he support himself?"

Frowning into the cup, she said, "As I say, I didn't know him then. I'm sorry I can't be of more help."

"How did you meet him?" Nell asked.

Again, Chloe took her time answering. "We had mutual acquaintances."

Will leaned forward on his elbows. "In the North End? Did you live there?"

"For a time." Looking up, Chloe said, "I'm sorry, but I can't see how things that happened so long ago could possibly have anything to do with...with what happened Tuesday night."

"If you know the North End," Will said, "that might be helpful to us in—"

"It's been ten years since I've lived there—no, eleven. There's nothing I can tell you about that area except that I hope to never see it again."

"We'll be heading up there tonight to look around and ask some questions," Nell said.

"You'd be better off doing it during the day," Chloe advised. "The darker it gets up there, the more vermin crawl out of the woodwork. Human vermin—though God knows there's plenty of the other kind, too."

Will said, "Yes, and the more information we're likely to come away with. Don't worry about Miss Sweeney. I won't leave her alone for a second."

"Have you ever been in the North End?" Chloe asked Nell.

"I attend mass at St. Stephen's."

"That's where Colin used to worship," Chloe said.

"Used to?"

"He's become disenchanted with the Church. He was a true son of Rome at one time. When he was young, he'd planned to become a priest."

"Really?" Nell pictured the big, gruff Irishman, with his meaty shoulders and giant head, celebrating mass in a chasuble and stole. Oddly enough, there was a certain rightness to the image.

"It was his mother's influence," Chloe said. "She thought he was special, different from his brothers. While the rest of them worked the mines from dawn till dusk, she made him spend a few hours every day at school. He'd been accepted into the seminary at Maynooth, but then came the uprising in 'forty-eight, and he had to flee the country. He'd already become a little distrustful of the Church because most of the clergy were so opposed to the Young Ireland movement, but he didn't stop attending mass till we lost little Patrick four years ago. Do you remember that old priest at St. Stephen's, the one Father Gorman replaced?"

"Father Keegan?"

"That's the one. He told Colin that Patrick couldn't be buried in holy ground, because he'd died unbaptized, and that he wasn't in Heaven, but in Limbo. Colin was…well, he was beside himself, furious. It was the final straw for him, the notion that an innocent babe could be tainted by sin before he was even born. He told Father Keegan that Patrick was with the angels no matter what he said, that the Church's laws weren't always God's laws, and that he'd worship with me from now on, at Emmanuel Church."

"Emmanuel?" Nell said. "You're Protestant?" It had never occurred to her; almost all of the Irish she'd met in Boston had been Catholic.

Chloe nodded. "Father Keegan married us very grudgingly, on the condition that our children be baptized in the Catholic faith and that Colin use his best efforts to convert me. He didn't—try to convert me, I mean. I'd been brought up Anglican, and he respected that. We did intend to bring our children up Catholic, until...Patrick. Colin told Father Keegan he wouldn't dream of raising our children in a church that had been so cruel to their own brother. I wasn't there, but he told me afterward that he said some things to Father Keegan that he wouldn't even repeat to me. Colin has quite a temper when he's roused."

"I don't think I've ever seen that side of him," Nell said.

"Neither have I—not directed at me, anyway, but I've seen him light into others." With a mordant little chuckle, Chloe said, "When they talk about getting your Irish up, they're talking about Colin. He must have made quite an impression, because Father Keegan had him excommunicated from the Church."

Nell's jaw literally dropped. "He's been *excommunicated?*"

"Ostensibly for holding beliefs against the Catholic faith, but really for making an enemy of Father Keegan."

"That must have been very upsetting to him. I mean, having wanted to be a priest at one time, and then having the Church reject him that way..."

"You know, it didn't really seem to trouble him too much. He said he knew in his heart that God still loved him, that it wasn't God rejecting him, it was just men who thought they had the right to speak on God's behalf, but really didn't."

From the corner of her eye, as she stared, dumbfounded, at Chloe, Nell saw Will turn to look at her. She knew he was recalling, as was she, his counsel last autumn—that if she were to remarry and be excommunicated, it would be the Church turning its back on her, not God. *God would never forsake you. You must know that.*

"Make no mistake," Chloe said, "Colin is still very much a believer, one of the best Christians I've ever met. He believes very strongly in living a good life, doing the right thing."

"I know," Nell said. "That's why I'm so sure he couldn't have committed this murder."

"If we knew more about the crime itself," Will said, "we'd be in a better position to sort through what happened."

"You said Constable Skinner paid a visit to you yesterday?" Nell asked.

Chloe groaned. "Around noon. I was frantic, wondering what had happened to Colin, and then that horrible little man showed up and told me about Cassidy being shot and Colin disappearing. He interrogated me for over an hour, and then he cornered Maureen in the kitchen and started in on her."

"Were you there for that conversation?" Nell asked.

Chloe shook her head. "He wouldn't let me stay, said he didn't want me 'exercising undue influence' over Maureen. She was shaking like a rabbit afterward, and wouldn't look me in the eye, so God knows what he said to her. I told her it wasn't true, about Colin being a murderer, but she didn't look convinced."

"What did Skinner question you about?" Will asked.

"Mostly he just wanted to know where Colin was. He didn't believe me when I said I didn't know, kept hammering at me, demanding the truth. He was terribly insulting, made some vile comment about…" She touched her stomach. "About Irish women dropping litters twice a year."

Will growled something under his breath.

"I kept my chin up," Chloe said. "I really didn't want to give that little insect the satisfaction of seeing me break down. It wasn't easy, though. Especially when he...well, when he told me about that woman being missing as well, and how Colin was supposed to have—"

"Woman?" Will said. "What woman?"

"Oh, God. I assumed you knew." Chloe dropped her head into her hands. "He...he told me Colin has a, a m-mistress in the North End. Mary something...Molloy. Mary Molloy."

"He didn't tell me this part," Nell said. "None of the details."

Drawing a deep breath, Chloe said, "This woman, she, she lives in a basement flat at Nabby's Inferno, with the man who was shot. They weren't married. Skinner called her his common-law wife. He said Colin..." She shook her head, fresh tears coursing down her cheeks.

Will handed her his handkerchief. "Take your time, Mrs. Cook."

"He...he said Colin had been visiting her for weeks, at night, w-when this Cassidy person wasn't home, and that he gave her money, and everyone knew they were...that he was—" She broke off on a sob.

Nell looked at Will, who grimaced and shook his head.

Taking Chloe's hand, Nell said, "Just because Skinner said it doesn't make it true. He's a vile man, he'd say anything. He was probably just trying to turn you against your husband so that you'd tell him where he is."

Struggling to regain her composure, Chloe said, "According to Skinner, it's common knowledge on North Street. That's where this Nabby's place is, near the corner of North and Clark, he said." Chloe gave her nose a final, sniffling wipe and refolded the handkerchief. "He said it's the biggest and most popular public house in that area, and the most notorious. He called it the black heart of Black Sea."

"The Black Sea?" Nell said.

"That section of the North End is the worst cesspool of crime and depravity in the city," Will said. "They call it the Black Sea—also the Murder District."

Chloe said, "Skinner told me Nabby's is where the worst of the worst gravitate for their drinking and gambling and—how did he put it?—'loose little bits of muslin like Mary Molloy.' He said there are people swarming in and around that place at all hours, and that Colin's been seen slipping out of her room. What they think happened Tuesday night is that Johnny Cassidy came home unexpectedly and caught Colin and Mary...in a compromising position, and that Colin ended up shooting Cassidy and taking her with him into hiding."

"Miss Sweeney is right to question Skinner's motives in telling you this," Will said, "if for no other reason than that he loathes your husband. Please try to put it out of your mind until we can go to this place and question some of these people ourselves."

"In the meantime," Nell added, "simply assume it's so much fabrication."

"I appreciate your concern over my feelings," Chloe said. "I truly do. But the fact is, I don't really care. I mean, I do care, of course. It hurts to think about it. I'm only human. He's my husband. I love him more than...than anything. He's my whole life. But the thing of it is, I know Colin feels the same way about me. I know it here." She pressed a hand to her heart. "If...if it's true, well, I hate it. But in a way, I can't really blame him."

"That's remarkably understanding of you," Will said.

"I wouldn't feel this way if it weren't for..." Chloe rested her hands on her stomach, a blush rising in her cheeks. "My doctor says I need to very careful if I'm to keep this baby, and...it's quite a bit for Colin to have to put up with."

"He's advised you to avoid marital relations?" Nell asked.

Chloe nodded, her blush deepening. "Colin says he doesn't mind. He says he loves me, and he loves the baby, and he only wants what's best for us. But he…he *is* a man, with a man's… natural inclinations."

"So you think he may have pursued those inclinations with Mary Molloy?" Will asked.

"If he did," Chloe said, "it…it wouldn't really have anything to do with me, and…how he feels about me. It wouldn't mean anything, not really. Like I said, I know he loves me, and I can't believe he feels the same way about her. All I really care about, all that's really important, is getting Colin back, and keeping him from hanging for murder. I c-couldn't bear to lose him. It would kill me."

Nell sat back, exhaling a pent-up breath.

"Mrs. Cook," Will said, "does your husband carry a gun?"

"Yes, of course, his Colt Police revolver. He always carries it when he's on duty."

"You wouldn't happen to know the caliber?" Will asked.

"Thirty-six," Chloe said. "I only know that because Skinner told me. He said the slug that was removed from Johnny Cassidy's head during the post-mortem yesterday morning looked to be about that size."

"Did he mention what kind of a wound it was?" Will asked. "Point blank? From a distance?"

"No," Chloe said. "Just that the bullet looked as if it came from Colin's gun."

"It could just as easily have come from any thirty-odd caliber revolver," Nell said, remembering their experience with the bullet they recovered from Virginia Kimball's bedchamber last summer. "Spent bullets get very misshapen. They're impossible to measure with any degree of accuracy."

"I *would* like to take a look at that wound," Will told Nell. "Unless the body's been buried already, which is unlikely, it should still be in the morgue at Massachusetts General. Why don't we stop by Isaac's office this afternoon and see if he can't arrange for us to have a peek?"

"Our friend Isaac Foster is assistant dean of the Harvard Medical School," Nell told Chloe. "Dr. Hewitt teaches there."

"Used to teach there," Will corrected, "which is why I'll have to go through Isaac to get into the morgue. I've lost my staff privileges." Leaning forward, he asked Chloe, "Just between the three of us, Mrs. Cook, do you think it's possible, even remotely, that your husband may have killed this man?"

Chloe's hesitation was telling. She looked from Will to Nell, and back again, then down at her hands. "I don't know what to think. All I really know is that he's my husband, and I love him, and I just want him back home with me, safe and sound. I don't care about…the rest of it. Whatever happened, it's all in the past. I just want him back."

CHAPTER SIX

"**D**EAR GOD," MURMURED EBENEZER SHUTE as he read Chloe Cook's succinct letter of introduction, in which she told him simply that her husband was a fugitive from a murder charge, that Nell and Will were trying to help him, and that they had her complete trust and confidence.

Shute had a trim build and dark, glossy hair combed back from a high forehead—not a bad looking fellow, despite some scar tissue near his left eye. The eye itself was artificial, but so beautifully made as to be almost undetectable. It was only the iris's lack of movement as Shute scanned the letter that betrayed it as glass.

"Poor Chloe." He shook his head, looking sobered and a little dazed by this turn of events. "When did this happen? Night before last?"

"That's right," said Will, seated next to Nell in one of a pair of high-backed leather chairs facing Superintendent Shute's desk in his homey, oak-paneled office. "This is the first you've heard of it?"

With a glum nod, Shute said, "I spent yesterday in Fort Hill, inspecting pawnshops, and today I've been holed up in here with a slew of paperwork. When the Detectives' Bureau was just down the hall, I knew everything that happened in this city—everything of a criminal nature, that is. Colin kept me well informed on a daily basis, and I must say there was a certain measure of diversion in that. Now…" He lifted his shoulders. "Days can go by without me interacting with anyone but my secretary."

"How often do you see Detective Cook?" Nell asked.

"Not as often as either of us would like, but it can't be helped. I work days, and Colin…well, I'm not sure what his official hours are, but he spends many an evening prowling the worst precincts of the city. We do meet from time to time in a tavern, and I've sneaked him into my club on occasion. He doesn't drink, but he doesn't mind being around it. And he and Chloe have me over to Sunday dinner at least once a month."

Nell said, "I'm surprised Constable Skinner hasn't come by today to question you about Detective Cook's whereabouts. He must realize what good friends you two are, after having worked in such close proximity to both of you."

"Of course he does," Shute said. "That's why he won't bother with me. He knows he could never convince me to part with information that might damage Colin. There would be no argument persuasive enough."

"Reasoned arguments aren't his modus operandi," Nell pointed out. "He'd most likely try to harass and browbeat you, as he did Mrs. Cook—and for that matter, me."

"I…think not," Shute said.

He seemed disinclined to elaborate, so Will, with his usual frankness, told her, "Skinner felt free to bully you and Mrs. Cook because you are not only female, but Irish, and therefore several levels lower than he in the almighty caste system that defines his life. Superintendent Shute, on the other hand, is several levels higher. As much as Constable Skinner might resent that, and I'm quite sure he does, he is essentially a gutless blowhard, and as such, would never dream of taking on his equals, much less his betters."

"Well put," Shute said with a smile. Leaning forward, he laid the letter on his desk next to an ornately carved cigar chest, to which his gaze strayed longingly. He glanced at Nell and sat back with a sigh.

"Oh, do light up," Nell said, then added what she often did when she wanted to set chivalrous gentlemen at ease. "I love the smell of a good cigar."

"Are you quite sure?" he asked.

"Please."

After offering a cigar to Will, who declined, Shute chose one and rose from his seat. He crossed to a tall, brocade-draped window, the knee joint of his wooden leg emitting a muffled clack-clack with each stiff-gaited step. Raising the window sash as high as it would go, he used a gold, pistol-shaped clipper hanging from his watch chain to slice off the tip of his cigar.

"Oh, dear," Nell said as Shute slid a match from a handsome enameled match safe and she caught a glimpse of his right palm, which bore an ugly, scabbed-over abrasion. "What happened to your hand, Superintendent?"

With a long-suffering smile, Shute displayed both palms to show that the left was similarly scarred. "I take the occasional tumble, I'm afraid. It's this fellow here," he said, knocking on the wooden leg through his trousers. "Can't do without him, but he's not what you'd call graceful. You should see me in the winter, when there's ice on the sidewalks. I'm covered in scrapes and bruises from November through March."

Will said, "I must say, Superintendent, you and Detective Cook seem like an odd pair to have ended up such good friends."

"We've got more in common than is immediately evident," Shute said as he lit his cigar. "We both almost became priests, for one thing." He shook out the match and tossed it into a marble ashtray on his desk.

Nell stared at him. "You…?"

Shute grinned. "I know. It comes as a shock to most people that I'm a Catholic. It's the name, I think—Ebenezer. It's Protestants who normally go in for the Old Testament names, but I was named after a family friend. Or perhaps it's that I'm a non-Irish Bostonian with a good job. Or perhaps it's the cut of my frock coat—who knows?"

She said, "Do you mind my asking why you didn't become a priest?"

Shute puff-puff-puffed on his cigar and blew a stream of smoke out the window. "Not temperamentally suited to it. I was a Jesuit seminarian, halfway through my studies at Woodstock College in Maryland, when I realized it would be a calamitous mistake for me to take holy orders. That life, the sacrifices…" He shook his head.

"Why did you pursue it in the first place?" Will asked.

"A reasonable question," Shute answered with a chuckle. "If only I'd asked it of myself at the time. The thing is, one of my older brothers, Nicholas, whom I idolized, had become a Jesuit priest. He went into teaching—he's headmaster of Georgetown Preparatory School in Bethesda now. I'd felt so alienated from the rest of my family, everyone but Nick. He was the only one I could talk to, the only one with whom I felt any rapport at all. If the Church was his vocation, of course it must be mine. That was my thinking, anyway. Simplistic, I know, but adolescent males tend to be simplistic creatures."

"So you left Woodstock College?" Will asked.

Shute nodded as he smoked his cigar. "Got a law degree at Harvard, which was when I fell in love with Boston. I went back home to start practicing. Well, not home, but close to it. I was taken on by a firm in Washington, D.C."

"When did you enlist in the Army?" Nell asked. It occurred to her, as the words were leaving her lips, that he hadn't told them about his service during the war; Chloe had. But there was the missing eye, the bum leg. Nell wondered how Shute would react to her query.

He smiled—one of those deep, wordless smiles that speak volumes. "I joined up as soon as war was declared. My parents were outraged—they and most of my siblings. They were slave owners, major supporters of the Maryland secession movement, in fact. My fighting for the Union, it was like a slap in the face. When I came home short a couple of body parts, they acted as if it was no more than I deserved for having defied them. So I moved back to Boston. I had friends here, fellows I'd gone to law school with. A couple of them were with the city government. That was how I ended up doing what I'm doing."

"Do you enjoy your work?" Will asked.

"I like going 'round to the pawnshops," Shute replied, "but the rest of it can get tedious at times. Sometimes I run up against a wall of bureaucratic twaddle and I wonder why I'm bothering. But it's a job that needs doing for the good of the city, and I do it well, so it's ultimately satisfying, and that's more than most men can say about their jobs."

"Do forgive the personal nature of the observation," Nell said, "but my understanding is that you have the means to be a man of leisure if you so desired."

"In other words, why do I choose to earn a living instead of living a life of parasitic entitlement?" Crossing with two halting steps to the desk, Shute rolled the tip of his cigar in an alabaster ashtray. "At the risk of oozing sanctimony, it's my opinion that if a man wants to hold his head up, he needs to be of some use to society, even in a small way. If that makes me self-righteous, you can blame the good Father Nick. He was the one who hammered that particular lesson into my head. 'Try to make a difference, Ben.' He must have told me that a hundred times—still does."

In that way, Nell reflected, Ebenezer Shute and Colin Cook were very much the same. She knew for a fact that Cook viewed law enforcement as a sort of mission to give malefactors their due. *I've got the comfort of having the good book on my side,* he'd told her once. *An eye for an eye, you know.*

Long before he joined the police department, there'd been something of the crusader about Cook—the Young Ireland Movement, organizing the mineworkers...Doomed endeavors, both. *Good intentions are no match for a little power.*

"Superintendent," she said, "I realize you didn't meet Detective Cook till after the war, and he'd been living here in Boston for a good decade before that, but do you happen to know what he did for a living when he first moved here? Not when he first got off the boat, but after he came back from Pennsylvania."

"Sure, he used to talk about it when he was in his cups—not so much anymore. He worked for Brian O'Donagh."

"Why do I know that name?" Nell asked.

"Oh, he's quite the big bug up in the North End," Shute said. "He and Colin came over on the same ship. They'd fought together in Ireland, and both escaped justice, such as it was, at the same time. Colin went off to mine coal in Pennsylvania, but O'Donagh stayed here and gathered together a group of Irishmen of like mind. Over the years, it's developed into quite a powerful organization. They call themselves the Fraternal Order of the Sons of Eire."

"I've heard of them," Nell said. "Aren't they...well, it's more or less a gang, isn't it?"

"Well, not in the sense of a pack of thugs stalking the streets with knives and brickbats. The Sons are always beautiful dressed and groomed. Oiled hair, silk cravats. They could pass for successful businessmen—which some of them actually are."

"But whenever I hear of them spoken of," Nell said, "it's always with a hint of fear."

"That wasn't always the case," Shute said. "According to Colin, the Sons were founded to fight discrimination against Boston's Irish, to help the men get jobs, and the women to feed their children. For the first few years, that's exactly what they did, but by the time I settled here, it was a different matter. They'd started using theft and violence to achieve their aims. They'd even use it against their fellow Irishmen if they didn't see eye to eye on something. And they started shaking down their constituents in the form of 'donations' to the cause. If you paid them off, you got protection. If you didn't, they were the ones you'd need protection from."

"And Cook worked for them?" Will asked.

"He said they weren't that corrupt yet when he took up with them in the mid 'fifties, at least not so much that he took exception to it—at first. O'Donagh recruited him as his lieutenant—his second in command, as it were. He was only with the Sons a few years. I know he was a constable by the time war was declared."

"Did he ever tell you why he parted ways with the Sons?" Will asked.

"Not in any detail. He said it was complicated, but I know he was disgusted with the road they were taking—the tactics, the payoffs."

Will said, "I would assume Cook runs across O'Donagh on a regular basis, seeing as he spends so much time in the North End. That's still where the Sons are headquartered, is it not?"

Nodding, Shute said, "Richmond Street, near Salem, in the back room of a pub called the Blue Fiddle that one of the Sons owns. I get the impression Colin tries to avoid running into O'Donagh."

"I should think it puts Cook in a fairly thorny position," Will said, "striving to maintain the law in a neighborhood where his old friend and compatriot is in the business of breaking it."

"O'Donagh's a smart man," Shute said. "He may be ultimately responsible for the actions of his men, but he's learned how to keep his hands clean—or at least, looking that way. Colin says it's virtually impossible to connect any criminal activity directly to him. As a state constable, he's expected to root out the sources of crime, but O'Donagh's been too slippery to pin down. In a way, Colin's been grateful for that. He doesn't relish the notion of having to arrest an old friend. On the other hand, he's a man of integrity, a man who embraces his responsibilities and always tries to do the right thing. That's why I'm just so incredulous at the notion that he's supposed to have killed a man. What made him a suspect in the first place?"

Will said, "We'll know more after we visit Nabby's Infero tonight, but—"

"Nabby's?" Shute looked up sharply.

"That's where the murder took place," Nell said. "Are you familiar with it?"

"It's infamous. And of course, I'm in that neighborhood quite a bit. There are half a dozen pawnshops on North Street that I monitor on a fairly regular basis."

"Have you been inside?" Will asked.

"Not my type of watering hole."

That wasn't precisely an answer, so Nell asked, "You never met Detective Cook there, even once, when you were in that area?"

"Um…well." Shute smiled a bit sheepishly. "As a matter of fact, we did run into each other on North Street the other evening—Monday, I believe. He was on his way there, so I tagged along."

"What was your impression of the place?" Nell asked.

"It's a snakepit. Can't say I'm surprised there's been a murder there."

"The victim was a fellow named Johnny Cassidy who lived at Nabby's," Will said. "He was shot in the head. I had the opportunity to examine the body before coming here, and it was apparent from the powder burns and other evidence that he was shot at close range, but not quite point blank. Shortly afterward, his common-law wife disappeared, along with Detective Cook."

Shute cocked his head as if he hadn't heard right. "What are you saying? Are you saying he took the woman with him?"

"It looks that way," Nell said. "Does the name 'Mary Molloy' ring any bells, Superintendent?"

He stared at her, smoke fluttering from his mouth. "Is that who he...Is...is that her name?"

"Yes. Do you know her?"

"No," Shute said. "No, I, uh, don't believe so."

"Detective Cook hasn't mentioned her to you?" Will asked.

Shute shook his head while studying his cigar with grave concentration.

Will said, "We've been told she's his mistress."

Shute gaped at them. "His *mistress?*"

"So we've been told," Nell said. "Please understand, Superintendent, we're trying to help him. Nothing you tell us will become public knowledge unless it's essential to keep him from hanging for a murder he didn't commit."

"He never told you about her?" Will asked.

"No," Shute said dazedly. "No, he...he wouldn't have."

"But you're his best friend, aren't you?" Nell asked.

"Yes, but Colin...He's the type of man who tends to hold his cards close to the vest when it comes to certain areas of his life. You know how it is. You disclose something to just one person, and that person lets it slip to someone else, and before you know it, you've spawned a world of heartache. He wouldn't never have risked telling me about a mistress. Colin loves Chloe more than anything in the world. He worships her. He'd rather die than hurt her. This Molloy woman, if it's true...I know she can't mean anything to him, not like Chloe does. I hope to God Chloe never finds out."

"She found out yesterday," Nell said.

"Oh, Christ." Shute sank back against the window sill, shaking his head. "That poor woman—and in her condition."

"You know about the pregnancy?" Nell asked.

With a rueful little smile, he said, "I know, I know. Colin wasn't supposed to tell anyone. And he didn't. As I said, he's discreet. But there's been something about his attitude of late, an excitement, a sense of anticipation. I guessed at the reason. He hesitated just long enough to confirm it. I was happy for him. His new position with the state constabulary has been more of a challenge than he'd anticipated, and he deserved some good news."

Nell said, "We understand you'd advised him to open his own private agency after the Detectives' Bureau was disbanded."

"Yes, and I wish he had. It would have been perfect for him. But he was concerned about providing for his family, and of course he was still reeling from the hearings and their aftermath. It's not easy to have the rug pulled out from under you, professionally, especially when you've done nothing to deserve it. He was an exemplary detective. Still is."

"Were you privy to the hearings at all?" Will asked.

"I wasn't present during them, but I followed them as closely as anyone, and I had my sources for information. Some of the men who were on the board that conducted the hearings belong to my club. Colin was found innocent of any serious misconduct, of course—in fact, as I understand it, the hearings pretty much showcased his sterling qualities, which was why Major Jones snapped him up for the state constabulary."

"Do you know anything about secret testimony Detective Cook may have given?" Nell asked. "Constable Skinner seems to think he fabricated evidence against them."

"I do know about that testimony," Shute said as he raised the cigar to his mouth. "It was about restructuring the city police. They just wanted Cook's candid opinion about what was wrong with the department and how to fix it."

"It had nothing to do with Skinner and his pals?" Will asked.

With a little grunt of humorless laughter, Shute said, "They didn't need Colin to condemn those men. Their offenses were many and varied—and well documented. I'm quite sure the only reason Skinner is still on the force is that he greased a few palms. Probably called in a few favors, maybe even engaged in a little blackmail."

"Whom would he have blackmailed?" Nell asked.

"One of the men overseeing the hearings, perhaps, someone in a position to say yea or nay to his continuing on the force. Cops learn all kinds of things about people, things men in certain positions wouldn't want known."

Shute leaned back against the wall, one hand in his pocket as he drew on his cigar. Through a drifting blur of smoke, he said, "Even the most upstanding among us have our little secrets, do we not?"

CHAPTER SEVEN

"**A** BIT WARM TONIGHT FOR THAT shawl, isn't it?" Will asked Nell as he handed her into a hackney on a dark street corner two blocks from Colonnade Row, where none of the Hewitts' neighbors would see them; he'd sold his phaeton and horses before leaving for Shanghai. "Nabby's Inferno," he told the driver as he climbed in next to her. "The corner of North and Clark."

Nell drew the swath of fringed wool around herself as she settled into the seat. "I think I may have overdone it."

Will had suggested they dress so as to blend in with the local denizens, the better to elicit their trust and cooperation. *If we show up at Nabby's looking like a couple of toffs on a gaslight tour of the slums, all we're likely to learn is how quickly they can pick us clean and hurl us back out onto the street.*

The only females who frequented North End saloons at night, Will had said, were those who either sold their favors outright, or in implicit exchange for shelter, protection, or trinkets. In that spirit, they tended to flaunt their charms rather boldly; a modestly attired lady would, paradoxically, attract a measure of suspicion after dark at a place like Nabby's.

There was no arguing with Will's logic. The only problem, aside from Nell's natural aversion to looking cheap, was the fact that she owned nothing that wasn't supremely tasteful; as a governess, it was incumbent upon her to present an image of refinement and good breeding. She'd resorted, finally, to rummaging through the clothing left behind by the Hewitts' maidservants when they departed for the Cape—the "civilian" garb they wore during their off hours. The pickings were slim. They'd taken most of it with them, of course, and there wasn't anything really tawdry—until Nell opened an old steamer chest belonging to one of her least favorite people, the cheeky, copper-haired Mary Agnes Dolan. Inside, she found three snug, lowcut basque bodices, a modish blue tournure skirt festooned with swags, ruffles and bows, a flashy little feathered hat, and a pair of fingerless black lace mitts.

Nell chose a basque of emerald satin, which was so wasp-waisted that she had to lace her stays within a quarter-inch of asphyxiation for it to fit. It was scandalously low-cut. She blanched when she looked down and saw how much bosom had been propped up on display. Reasoning that exhibition was, after all, the idea, she resolved to throw herself into the role, rouging her lips and cheeks and twisting her hair into a loose chignon with ringlets haloing her face and tumbling down her nape. Her accessories were a mesh reticule, some of Mary Agnes's paste necklaces, the feathered hat, and the mitts.

She'd smiled at her reflection in the mirror on the Hewitts' entryway hallstand, thinking, *If Saint August could see me like this...*The grin vanished when she heard Will come in through the back door, having returned from a visit to his house to collect his things. She snatched one of Viola's shawls off the hat rack and hastily wrapped it around herself, wishing she'd thought to pin a lace fichu over her décolletage. It would have compromised the effect, of course, but at least she could have held her head up.

Turning toward Nell on the seat of the hack, Will—clad in a humble sack coat and tweed cap—said, "I can't imagine you've gone too far. You may think you have, given that monstrous propriety of yours, but some ladies are incapable of true vulgarity, and you're one of them. Come, now." He pushed the shawl off her shoulders. "You're supposed to look like a tart tonight, not a school..." He blinked down at her. "Marm."

"You see?" she said, pulling the shawl back up.

He tugged it back down. "Nell, don't be ridiculous. It's far too warm a night for—"

"But I look…I look…"

"You look wonderful," he said softly.

"I'll be plagued by leering boors," she said. "They'll stare at my…" She glanced down at her abundant cleavage.

"Any man you'll encounter at a place like Nabby's is used to seeing women dressed like that. They won't leer."

"It's just…it's been a long time since I've fit in with people like this. I've gotten so far from these people, this world. It feels…" She shook her head.

"I know." Will closed his hand over hers, but withdrew it almost immediately, as if he'd committed some sort of indiscretion. "It's not as if you're returning to this world, though, not really. You're just acting a part, for Colin Cook's sake."

"And his wife's. Poor woman. I can't imagine what she's going through."

Will said, "You do realize she's hiding something."

Nell just sighed.

"All that elusiveness about how they first met," he said.

"I know."

"And this mysterious favor she wrote to thank him for."

"I know, I know."

"In other respects, I thought she was admirably forthcoming—except when I asked her outright if she thought her husband could have killed Johnny Cassidy. I mean, I like her—quite a lot, actually—but it does make me wonder."

"I still can't help but feel sorry for her, being ambushed that way by Skinner, and in her condition. He didn't have to tell her all that, about her husband and Mary Molloy."

"Do you suppose it's true?" Will asked.

"I don't know. I really don't. On the one hand, he's always spoken so lovingly of her. But on the other, well…like she said, he *is* a man, and men…"

"And men…?" He was fighting a smile, the dog.

She cast him a baleful look. "Have needs."

"Ah, yes, those primitive, ravenous needs of ours. It has actually been my observation that if a man is truly devoted to his wife, and if he's mature enough to have sorted out that one can't eat one's cake and have it, he can and will remain faithful through thick and thin—even if it means doing without the pleasures of the marital bed for months, or longer."

"Nevertheless," Nell said, "men do occasionally stray, even good men like Detective Cook. If we start out by assuming he didn't, we might miss something important."

"You dodged that assumption very adroitly," Will said with a hint of a smile. "My incessant hectoring has borne fruit, after all." Tapping on the roof of the cab, he told the driver to pull over.

"Nabby's is a block away in that direction," he said as he handed Nell down from the carriage and paid the driver. "It's probably best if we're not seen getting out of a hack by the people we'll be dealing with. Mustn't look too prosperous."

He took her arm and escorted her up North Street, a meandering cobblestone lane lined with tenements and shopfronts, each more dismal and ramshackle than the last. Men swaggered down the sidewalk in packs, snorting with laughter as they drank from their flasks and smoked their cigarettes. Frowsy streetwalkers clustered beneath the lamp posts, fanning their sweat-sheened, desperately painted faces. The balmy night air carried whiffs of spoiled fruit, sewage and sour ale, underscored by the musty-damp smell of Boston Harbor just to the east.

"This is it," Will said as they approached a weathered brick building fronted with leaded glass windows glowing orange-yellow in the dark. Men and women milled about in front, flirting and laughing, smoking and drinking. From within came muffled, lively piano music.

"Have you ever been here?" Nell asked Will.

"A few times, many years ago, but just for the drinking, never to play cards." Lowering his voice so as not to be heard by those loitering nearby, he said, "Even back then, I knew enough not to wager a dime here. It's a skinning joint. They've got their hands in your pocket from the moment you set foot in the place. If a man walks in alone, he's immediately set upon by a bar girl who asks him for a dance—for which he has to pay, of course. Then she'll be thirsty and want a drink, which, although it contains no alcohol, will set the chump back a pretty penny. Then comes the invitation to go off to some private nook for a more intimate form of entertainment, which will cost him whatever is left in his wallet. The card games are crooked, the boxing is fixed..."

"Boxing?"

"A couple of nights a week, they set up a boxing ring in the dance hall at the rear of the building and have bare-knuckled matches. The other nights, it's music and dancing."

He led her to a cluster of dusty, framed photographic portraits hanging in Nabby's front window facing the glass, so that they could be viewed from outside by the light of a nearby street lamp. The photographs on top were of powerfully built, shirtless men scowling at the camera, fists raised. Each picture had a name inked across the bottom in a spikey scrawl: *Phelix McCann, Davey Kerr, Pat "Bulldog" Cunigan, Jimmy Muldoon, Finn "Southpaw" Cassidy, Johnny Cassidy...*

"Look," Nell said, pointing to the photos of the two men named Cassidy, who bore a striking resemblance to each other, although one was dark, the other fair. The dark one, the late Johnny, was captured in a boxer's crouch, fists curled near his face.

He was turned away from the camera, the three-quarter profile highlighting his heavy brow and sharp cheekbones. Finn Cassidy, although he shared Johnny's rapacious features, was substantially bigger than Johnny, a hulking brute with bulging muscles and small eyes cast into shadow beneath his brow ridge. Both men looked to be in their early to mid-thirties.

"Brothers?" Nell said.

"Looks like it. Those must be the wenches who work here," Will said, indicating the dozen or so photographs below those of the boxers. They were full-length portraits of young, suggestively attired women, some in just their underpinnings, striking seductive poses. They had been labeled with first names only: *Flora, Ivy, May, Pru, Fanny, Elsie, Mary…*

"Do you suppose that's Mary Molloy?" Nell asked, pointing.

"She's the only Mary there."

"I didn't realize she worked here."

"I assumed she did."

The girl in the photograph looked young, very young, an effect emphasized by her petite stature and juvenile attire. Unlike the other bar girls, she wore a modest, white-collared blue frock hemmed above the ankles, displaying a pair of dainty black boots, a peek of white stocking, and a lacy fringe of petticoat. She had little in the way of bosom, but the face of an angel, with huge, pale eyes, a turned-up nose, and bee-stung lips. Her hair, which Nell guessed, from her befreckled complexion, to be red, fell over her shoulders in a torrent of ringlets.

"She doesn't look old enough to be someone's common law wife," Nell observed, "not to mention a…Well, I take it these women are essentially prostitutes."

"Some men have a taste for young girls," Will said. "They're usually immature themselves, and looking for someone they can control."

"It surprises me that Johnny Cassidy could have tolerated her selling herself to other men."

"It may very well have been his idea," Will said. "Easy money."

"Easy for *him*."

Will gestured her through the front door, where a muscular, reddish-blond man in a tweed vest, but no coat, halted them with an upraised hand. He had the faded remnants of a black eye and a somewhat fresher contusion on his forehead. Nell recognized his deepset eyes and feral features from the photograph in the window.

"Two bits for you," he told Will in a voice that bore just the faintest hint of an Irish lilt. "The lady gets in free."

"You're Finn Cassidy, ain't you?" Will asked in a passably good working class Boston accent. *You don't show up at an Irish grogshop sounding like a Brit to the manor born,* he'd told her, *and expect them to welcome you with open arms.* Digging in his pocket for the twenty-five cents, he said, "Sorry 'bout what happened to your brother."

"Did you know him?" Finn asked.

"No, but I—"

"No, you don't, Boyle," Finn growled as a grubby, boozy-smelling behemoth tried to squeeze through the doorway past Nell and Will. He pounced on Boyle with surprising alacrity, given his bulk, and seized him by his suspenders.

"But I ain't so bollocksed now," Boyle said in a heavily slurred brogue, trying to pry Finn's grip loose as he was shoved out of the door and onto the sidewalk. "And I din' really hurt her, not so's she'd feel it tomorrah. I won' do it again, I swear."

"Not tonight, you won't." Finn gave the interloper a rough shove, sending him stumbling backward into the lamp post. The crowd loitering on the sidewalk hooted with laughter.

Finn said, "You know the rules, Boyle. Once I give you the heave-ho, you're out for the night. Come back tomorrow and don't give the chippies no trouble, and maybe I'll let you stay."

"Och, Finn, be a good lad," Boyle implored as he lurched back toward the door, straightening his coat. "Lemme back in, jus' fer tonight, and I swear on me dear departed mum's—"

He broke off with a grunt as Finn grabbed him by the collar and rammed his left fist into his gut, doubling him over. The onlookers, appreciating the impromptu floor show, whooped and cheered. A second punch, this one to the head, dropped Boyle in a groaning heap on the sidewalk, blood streaming from his nose.

Nell instinctively stepped forward, ready to intervene, as Finn aimed a booted foot at the fallen man's midsection, but Will pulled her back, tucking her behind him. "Bad idea," he said quietly, but she could tell from his stance of coiled readiness that he was prepared to step in himself if need be.

The kick connected with a muffled crunch and a roar of pain.

Turning to leave, Finn said, "Not another word from you, you hear?"

"Christ Jaysus," Boyle rasped, clutching his stomach.

Wheeling around, Finn dealt the big man another kick, then brought his boot down on Boyle's throat and kept it there, making him gag and thrash. Leaning over, he asked, with studied calm, "Now, what did I say? 'Not another word.' That means you close that flappin' jaw of yours and keep it closed. Got it?"

A gurgle rose from Boyle's throat as he stared, bug-eyed, at his tormenter.

"Got it?" Finn repeated, bearing down with his foot.

Boyle nodded jerkily.

Finn kept it up another few seconds, regarding his victim with undisguised contempt, before easing up and backing away. "Get him out of my sight," he told no one in particular. Several men scrambled to do his bidding as he turned back to Will, holding out a big, scarred hand, palm up. "Two bits."

Will paid him, shoved his cap into a pocket of his jacket, and guided Nell into the saloon. "So. Finn Cassidy bounces as well as boxes."

"Bounces?"

"Keeps order, throws out the trash. No small task in a place like this."

"That doesn't give him the right to such savagery."

"Such savagery is a nightly occurrence in places like this," said Will, "a fact of which Mr. Boyle was certainly well aware when he did whatever it was he did to get him ejected in the first place. More to the point, though, if I'd allowed you to call Finn Cassidy on the carpet for exercising his professional responsibilities as he sees fit, how willing do you think he would have been to grant us entrance to this place?"

"I know, but…" Nell shuddered, remembering the sickening crunch of those ribs. She'd softened over the years. Back when she was part of this world, or one very like it on Cape Cod, she'd had a thicker skin. On the one hand, it shamed her that she couldn't handle things she used to be able to. On the other, her newfound delicate sensibilities were part of what defined her as a lady by the standards of Boston's elite. They accepted her as one of their own—*almost,* but it was a good deal more than she'd ever had before.

Curling an arm around her waist, Will whispered, "We must keep our eye on our goal, Cornelia. We came here for information. We came for Colin Cook, to keep him from hanging. Nothing else matters."

She nodded, sucked in a deep, calming breath, and looked around.

Nabby's Inferno was housed in a building whose rooms—those on the first floor, anyway—had been mostly stripped of their walls, while retaining distinctly different ceilings and floors.

In the front stood a long bar set up with kegs of beer and whiskey to serve the patrons sitting at, or slumped over, a hodgepodge of mismatched tables. A kaleidoscope of smoke-hazed mirrors, photographs, nude paintings, ribald engravings, and newspaper clippings adorned the walls. Nell breathed in a miasma of stale booze, staler sweat and cheap tobacco that made the gorge rise in her throat.

Toward the rear of the establishment was a dance floor and a stage, on which a man with lampblack hair and a faded dinner jacket leaned on a piano while crooning "The Man on the Flying Trapeze" between sips of what looked like whiskey. A few sailors were dancing with girls Nell recognized from the photographic display out front, while other customers—a diverse mix from all elements of Boston society, high and low—milled about, listening to the music or talking over it. On one corner of the stage three women in garish face paint and frothy can-can skirts sat sharing a cigarette, their black-stockinged legs nonchalantly dangling over the edge.

Catching the attention of a straw-haired waiter girl passing by with two pitchers of beer, Will asked her who they should see about renting a room. "That'd be Riley," she said, nodding toward the bartender, a thickset fellow with a steel wool beard.

"We ain't no boarding house," Riley told them as he wiped out a used glass with a soiled rag and set it with the "clean" ones. "What makes you think we got rooms to let?"

"I heard you got a basement flat that just opened up," Will said. "The guy that lived there kicked the bucket is what I heard."

"You just want a place to live, or you got somethin' else in mind?"

"If we just wanted a place to live," Will said with a snide little smile, "I reckon we could find lots quieter places than this."

Riley looked Nell up and down in a way that made her wish she'd kept herself covered up with the shawl, his gaze stilling for a long moment when it lit on her bosom. When he turned away to bellow "Flora!" to a plump bar girl, Nell gave Will an I-told-you-so look.

He just smiled and shrugged. She hiked her shawl up over her shoulders. He pulled it back down. "When in Rome, Cornelia…"

"I got to take these two to see Mother," Riley told the bar girl. "Keep an eye on the hooch—and your nose out of it."

"Don't be long," she said as she sauntered over. "It's been a slow night for me, and my rent's overdue. I gotta get busy."

The bartender strode through the saloon with Nell and Will on his heels until he came to a room at the very rear, the only one whose walls were still intact. "Wait here," he told them as he passed through the open doorway.

The room was large, dim, and choked with cigar smoke. Men, some with bar girls draped over them, sat at three round, oilcloth-covered tables playing cards. The only other furniture in the room was a writing desk facing the door, behind which, on a velvet-upholstered, barrel-back wing chair, sat the largest woman Nell had ever seen.

Her body was colossal, a half-ton of bread dough ballooning out of a sleeveless linen garment that looked suspiciously like an undershift. As a nod to modesty, she wore over it a blue-striped pinafore, its gathered yoke only accentuating her size while imparting a grotesque air of the infantile. The skirt ended several inches above the floor, revealing splayed feet clad in unlaced men's brogans, the flesh oozing over them in flabby rolls. Were it not for her unbound hair, brown and lank but threaded with wiry gray filaments, she would have looked for all the world like a giant's baby doll. Young, she wasn't; yet she certainly didn't have enough years on her to be Riley's mother.

"Mother Nabby," Riley said with a nod of greeting as he approached her. Leaning down close, he spoke too softly for

Nell to hear above the applause from the adjacent dance hall. The vocalist announced that his next tune would be "Molly! Do You Love Me?" whereupon several audience members screamed, "Beautiful Dreamer! Beautiful Dreamer!" "I bow to public sentiment," he said, and launched into that song instead.

Riley glanced in their direction, whereupon Mother Nabby did the same. Her tiny eyes, like raisins pushed into the pale, damp mound of her face, moved over the two of them in dispassionate appraisal. She raised a clay pipe to her mouth, took a puff, and blew out a contemplative plume of smoke. Unlocking a desk drawer with a key hanging around her neck, her massive arms wobbling like jelly, she retrieved a large anchor-shaped keyring with two old iron keys on it. She handed it to Riley, saying something to him.

"Denny!" Riley barked.

A boy Nell hadn't noticed before jumped up from the floor in the corner, a book in his hand. He was a gangly youth of about fourteen, with overgrown hair and shabby clothes, good-looking despite his skinniness and a misshapen nose that was probably the result of a poorly healed fracture.

"Take these folks downstairs and show 'em the flat," Riley said as he tossed the key ring across the room to Denny.

The boy reached out to catch it, but fumbled, wincing when it struck his hand. As he scooped it off the floor, Nell saw that the middle and index fingers of his right hand were crooked, the knuckles distended.

"Mary and Johnny's place?" Denny asked as he tucked the book into the waist of his trousers in back. "How come?"

"Stop askin' so many questions and start earnin' your keep," said Mother Nabby in a husky rumble as she relocked the drawer.

"Since he's going downstairs," Riley told Mother. "I could use some Jameson's."

Shooting Riley a look of disgust for making her unlock the drawer again, Mother withdrew a shiny brass key tied to a red ribbon, and gave it to him. "Anything else?" she asked snidely.

"No, ma'am. Sorry to trouble you. Here." He said, handing the key to Denny. "Bring me back a jug of Jameson's from the coal cellar. Be sure and lock it up after, and come right back up. No holin' up down there in a corner with your nose in that book. You hear me, boy?"

"Start earning your keep?" Denny grumbled as he led Nell and Will through the saloon toward the basement stairwell. "Any errand they got, no matter what it is, I hop to it. Nobody ever gave me nothin' I didn't work for, ever."

"Where d'you think you're goin' with them keys, you little shite?" It was Finn Cassidy, striding toward them with an expression of fury.

CHAPTER EIGHT

B ACKING UP, DENNY SAID, "R-RILEY wants me to fetch him a jug of Jameson's from—"

"Not that key." Pointing to the anchor-shaped key ring, Finn said, "Those."

"I, um, I'm s'posed to take these folks downstairs and show 'em Mary and Johnny's flat."

"We're thinking of renting it," Will said.

"The hell you are," Finn said. "My brother ain't even cold yet. I ain't got the place emptied out. All his stuff's still in there. Gimme that," he ordered, reaching for the key ring.

"Mother says I got to show it to 'em," Denny told Finn in a shuddering voice as he held the keys behind his back. "I don't do what she says, she'll toss me right back out on the street. You know that."

His hands squeezing into fists, Finn snarled, "You don't do what *I* say, I deal you a few more cracked bones—big ones this time, arms and legs. You wanna end up a cripple, or you wanna give me them keys?"

Stepping between the hulking Finn and the cowering boy, Will said, "The kid's just following his boss's orders. She's your boss, too, ain't she?"

"You stay outa this," said Finn, stabbing a finger in Will's face. "This ain't none of your affair."

Tell you what," Will said, pressing a coin into Finn's hand. "Why don't you take it up with Mother Nabby, and meanwhile we'll just have a quick look at the room. We may not even want it."

Finn studied the coin, a gold half eagle, with a surly but covetous expression before slipping it in his pocket. "I know everything that's in that room," he told Denny. "You pinch somethin', you even just *touch* somethin', and you'll answer to my fists. Same goes for you," he told Will. Turning, he stalked off toward the back room and Mother Nabby.

Denny let out a weighty sigh and turned to Will, "Thanks, mister. Finn, he's..." He shook his head.

"A real hard chaw, eh?" Nell asked.

"He's the Devil himself," the boy said grimly as he watched Finn disappear into the back room. "Meanest pug I ever knew."

Will said, "He's the one who broke your nose and your fingers, is he?"

Denny's jerked his shoulders, his gaze on the floor.

"How come?" Will asked.

Denny's gaze shifted from Will to Nell, then back to the floor. "I reckon he was riled up. That there's the basement stairs," he said before Will could question him further. "I'll go first. You want to be watchin' your step, miss. Couple of these stairs are loose, and it's dark as Hades till you get to the bottom."

As they descended the stairwell, a sweetly scorched aroma wafted up from below, almost like molasses burnt to the bottom of a pan—but with a telltale, underlying muskiness. Nell shared a look of recognition with Will when they got to the bottom of the stairs.

"Where's the hop joint?" Will turned to survey the basement, a cool, dimly lit cavern with stone-block walls and a ceiling so low that he had to duck under the beams as he walked.

The boy pointed toward a shadowy corner, where there was a doorway hung with a glass-beaded curtain, dark within but for the flicker of oil lamps. "That's where they smoke it. Two bits for a pipeful. It's my job to check up on 'em and fetch more gong from Mother when they want it. She keeps it locked up in her desk."

"What's are those for?" Nell asked, pointing to a row of four small, curtained-off alcoves. From behind one of them came a woman's muffled voice.

"Those are, um…" Denny glanced at Nell, then at Will, whose smile alerted her to the naïveté of her question, which she suddenly wished she could take back. Even in the subterranean gloom, she could see the blood rise in Denny's cheeks. "We call 'em the dance booths, 'cause they're for when a customer wants to be alone with one of the girls for a…private dance."

"Yes, of course," Nell said, her own cheeks stinging for having been a source of such amusement for Will. Only he had ever been able to make her blush like that.

"There's more booths up on the second floor," Denny said, "plus a couple of rooms tricked out all special for the swells that want somethin' a little fancier. Course, they cost a lot more."

"Mother Nabby certainly makes this place pay," Will said.

"You wouldn't know it to look at her," Denny said, "but she's prob'ly the richest woman in the North End. She don't have just this place. She's got her thumb in lots of pies around here, and she's a lot smarter than you'd think. Not the nicest lady I ever met, but she knows how to make a nickel." Plucking a lantern off a hook on one of the rafters, he said, "Mary and Johnny's flat is back through here, by the coal cellar."

Denny guided them through the dank warren to the back of the building, where there were two doors with peeling green paint, side by side. The left one had a tarnished old lock plate, the right, a gleaming padlock. Twisting one of the keys in the lefthand door, he opened it and ushered them inside. A deathlike mustiness greeted them, overshadowing the smell of burning opium.

"It's just the one room?" Nell asked, looking around.

"Yeah. Sorry." Denny set the lantern down on a table draped with a stained, checkered cloth and lit a candle. Laid out on the table were playing cards arranged in a game of solitaire and a cup containing the evaporated remnants of what appeared to have been tea. From the look of the cards, the game had been interrupted halfway through. The ladderback chair at which the player had sat lay on its back in the middle of the stone floor near a rumpled-up braided rug.

A bed stood against the rear wall beside a weathered old wardrobe, its doors so warped from dampness that they didn't meet anymore. From the looks of the threadbare quilt tucked over the bed, it had been tidily made up, then tousled, as if someone—or, more likely, a couple—had used it without unmaking it.

The walls were marred with water stains, mildew, and innumerable networks of cracks. Whole chunks of plaster were missing, exposing raw stone on the two outside walls, and rotted wooden lath on the others. The righthand wall, above a scarred old sea chest, bore a dark, ominous stain—a brownish-red burst surrounded by tiny spatters. There was more blood on the chest, against which Johnny Cassidy must have fallen, and a pool of it on the floor where he'd presumably come to rest.

"That will take some cleaning," Nell said.

"Yeah, the, uh, the fella that lived here before," Denny said, "he got shot in the head a couple of nights ago. Shot dead."

"We heard about that," Will said. "Johnny Cassidy, right?"

"Yeah, him and Mary Molloy lived here."

"What happened to her?" Nell asked.

"She's gone."

"Gone where?" Will asked.

The boy shrugged, shaking his head and looking everywhere but at Will. "Nobody knows. She run off after Johnny got killed."

"What makes you so sure she ran off?" Nell asked. "If a murder took place here, perhaps she was the victim of foul play. She could have been taken against her will, or harmed in some way."

"Nah," he said, shaking his head at the floor. "It wasn't nothin' like that. I mean…I sure hope it wasn't."

"If you know where she is," Will said, "I wish you'd tell us. We wouldn't want her showing up and wanting her flat back after we've moved in."

"I wish I did know," Denny said. "I been worried about her."

"You like her?" Nell said.

The boy reddened violently. "She's all right."

"I saw her picture out front," Nell said. "She's very pretty."

Denny's Adam's apple bobbed. Lifting the lantern, he said, "You, uh, seen enough, or…?"

"Does that lead to outside?" Will asked, pointing to a door on the back wall next to a small, curtained window near the ceiling.

"Oh. Yeah." Carrying the lantern over to the door, Denny unlocked it and pulled it open with a grind of corroded hinges, revealing a narrow flight of stone walkout steps. "You got your own outside entrance if you want. You don't have to go through the saloon to get in here."

"What's out here?" Will asked as he climbed the stairs, with Nell and Denny on his heels. "The stable?"

"No stable. Just the privy and the old chicken house, which is where Finn lives."

"He lives in a chicken house?"

"He fixed it up."

By the light of a waxing half-moon, Nell could see that the backyard was small and overgrown with scrubby weeds, save for a beaten-down path leading from the side alleyway to the basement stairwell. The privy was built of wood, the chicken house of stone with a double wooden door and a row of shuttered windows. To the right of the basement stairs was the little flat's narrow window, its glazing filthy and cracked, to the left a coal chute with a rusty metal door. From its size and shape, she guessed that it had once been another window.

From inside the dance hall came a round of applause, and then someone yelled, "Bring on the girls!" Other men repeated the demand, to the accompaniment of whistles and the stomping of feet.

"Is this outside door always kept locked?" Nell turned toward Denny to find him hastily averting his gaze from her chest. She shot a look at Will, who appeared to be biting back a smile.

"Um, yeah." Denny shrugged without meeting her gaze. "I mean, I reckon so. Mary and Johnny had the keys. I guess they prob'ly would have locked it, what with the type of roughnecks that hang around here. I know *I* would have."

"Does Mother Nabby have duplicate keys to those?" Will asked. "Others that open the same locks?"

"Yeah, sure, she's got extras for every door. She's got about a million of keys in that drawer of hers. And I know what 'duplicate' means. I ain't...I'm not dumb. I had seven years of schooling. Just the public school, but I never missed a day, not one."

A roar of cheers from inside drowned out the opening bars of the pianist's new tune. When the ovation died down, Nell recognized the rousing "Galop Infernal" from Offenbach's operetta *Orphee aux Enfers.*

"Do you still go to school?" Nell asked Denny.

"Nah. My mum and sister caught the smallpox a couple of years ago, and went to their rest. I had to start lookin' after myself then. Runnin' errands for Mother, I get food and a place to sleep. It's this or the poor house, and I ain't livin' in no poor house."

"I don't blame you," Nell said with heartfelt sincerity.

"I work for my keep," Denny said with feeling. "I'm a Delaney. My mum always said us Delaneys never took a cent of charity from anyone, and I never will."

"Do you miss school?" Nell asked, thinking about that book he'd had his nose in earlier.

"It was all right." He looked away, shifting his jaw. "Yeah, sure. I liked it well enough. I mean, I liked the reading and writing, and learning about different countries, but I didn't much care for them stuck-up…those stuck-up schoolmarms. They treated us Irish kids like dirt. During morning prayers, we had to say 'em the Protestant way, and we couldn't make the sign of the cross, or we'd get a whack with the yardstick. They said we were ignorant foreigners, and we had to learn to do things the right way, but then Father Gorman would say *our* way was the right way, and *they* were wrong."

"I imagine it was pretty confusing," Nell said.

"Not for me. I'm a Catholic. My folks were Catholic, and their folks, and their folks, goin' back hundreds and hundreds of years. I don't ever want to be nothin' else. They could make me say different words, those schoolmarms, but they couldn't ever change what I am in here." He thumped his chest with a dirt-smudged finger.

"Good for you," Nell said, feeling a twinge of envy for his conviction, his unassailable fealty to his religion. She'd shared that fealty herself once, that comforting certainty that her Church's way was *the* way. She never thought she'd feel any other way, yet here she was, contemplating not just Protestantism, but divorce.

They went back inside and inspected the flat a while longer, vainly searching for some indication as to what had happened there Tuesday night. Through the ceiling came the rhythmic thudding of the can-can dancers' feet as they kicked and gyrated on the stage directly overhead.

"Um…I don't think you should really be doin' that," Denny said when Nell cracked open the door to the wardrobe.

"I just wanted to see how much room there is inside for my things," Nell said. "The furniture does come with the flat, doesn't it?"

"I dunno. All's I know is, Finn'll trounce me good if he finds out I let you look through Mary and Johnny's stuff. I'm sorry, really, but—"

"It's not important," said Will, aiming a trenchant glance at Nell as he crossed to the door. "I think we've seen enough to make a decision, so we may as well…" Turning back to Denny, he said, "Oh, wait. Don't you have to fetch something for the bartender? A jug of Jameson's, was it?"

"Oh, yeah. Thanks. I almost forgot. Riley woulda chewed me out somethin' fierce." Digging the key with the red ribbon out of his trouser pocket, he said, "It's in the coal cellar next door. I'll be right back."

He left with the lantern, plunging the room into darkness save for a trembling corona of light around the candle on the table. Will crossed to the sea chest and flipped up its lid. Nell opened the wardrobe and began rummaging through its paltry, oft-mended contents: three men's shirts, two pair of trousers, a sack coat, a vest, torn suspenders, two pairs of darned socks, two shirt collars, a striped cravat, soft lace-up boots, a wide canvas belt with a leather buckle, and a pair of light gray, form-fitting knitted trousers similar to dancers' tights. She recognized the boots, trousers and belt from Johnny Cassidy's photograph in the window.

"Did you wear this sort of thing when you boxed for Oxford?" she asked Will.

He looked up from the sea chest, through which he was hurriedly rooting. "I did, yes. Quite cozy, actually, except for the belt. There's nothing very remarkable in here, some moth-eaten blankets, a bit of this and that."

"Well, there's one remarkable thing about what's in here," she said. "It's all Johnny Cassidy's. There's not one item of female clothing in this wardrobe. No hats, jewelry, shoes, stockings, underthings—nothing."

"Which would suggest," Will said as he closed the chest, "that she packed her things before leaving."

"Which, in turn, would suggest that she left voluntarily."

"Well, that's something, I suppose." Looking around, he muttered, "Bloody miserable place to call home. Excuse the language."

Nell nodded as she closed the wardrobe. "Like living in a cave. Must be worse in the winter. I can't imagine…" She trailed off, squinting across the room at a glimmer of light high on the wall that separated the flat from the coal cellar.

"What is it?" Will asked as Nell crossed the room to take a closer look.

"There's a hole here." Standing on tip-toe, she reached up to trace the outline of the little aperture, which was about as big around as a man's thumb. It blended in so well with the blackish speckles of mildew near the ceiling that she would never have noticed it had Denny not taken that lantern into the coal cellar.

Coming up behind her, Will said, "It's hardly surprising there should be a hole in one of these walls. It looks as if they've been deteriorating for years."

"This doesn't look like the product of deterioration," she said, stepping aside so that he could see what she meant. "It's the only gap in a pretty solid expanse of plaster, and look—it's almost perfectly round, and neat, unnaturally so."

"As if someone had chiseled it out deliberately," Will said.

"Do you think it could be some kind of…spy hole?"

"Let's go take a look from the other side."

CHAPTER NINE

THE COAL CELLAR, WHICH WAS about half the size of the adjacent flat, also had crumbling plaster walls, gone dusky from years' worth of coal dust. Tucked into the back left corner, beneath the chute, a rudimentary coal crib had been built out of rough, unfinished wood. Within this three-sided enclosure a small mound of coal left over from the winter glittered darkly in the wavering light from Denny's lantern.

A coal shovel and a broom missing about half its bristles leaned against the back wall amid a grimy accumulation of detritus: shards of wood and crockery, a coil of twine, some wadded up handkerchiefs, an unidentifiable, lace-edged lady's undergarment, old newspapers and magazines, a torn burlap sack, and an empty bottle of McMunn's Elixir. There was also something that looked like a fat test tube made of rubber, which Nell assumed was a French letter, although she'd never actually seen one. Both fascinated and repelled, she tried not to stare, lest Will notice and tease her about it later—anything to coax a blush out of her.

Piled up against the wall to the right was a jumble of wooden crates, barrels, and sacks, which Denny was busily searching through as he held the lantern aloft.

"Aha!" He hauled a stoneware jug stamped *John Jameson Dublin Whiskey* out of a crate lined with wood shavings. "What are you doing?" he asked as Will climbed atop the coal crib's low wooden partition, rather gracelessly, given his bad leg.

Will bent over, arms buttressed on the wall, to peer through the hole, all but invisible against the haze of coal dust.

"We discovered a hole between this room and the flat," Nell said.

"You get a pretty fair view from here," Will said in his Boston accent. "The hole is angled downward, so I can see a good deal of the room."

"Did you know about this hole?" Nell asked Denny.

He stared at her for a second. "Um…no. No, I…" He shook his head.

"It's a hole for peeking into the flat," Will said. "Someone bored it out for that very purpose. Denny, hand me that lantern, would you?"

Still balancing on the edge of the coal crib, Will took the lantern and held it toward the hole. The wall surrounding it bore smudges in the patina of coal dust. Scores of smeary handprints formed fluttery, ghostlike wings to either side.

"Any idea who might have made that hole?" Nell asked Denny. "*I* didn't."

"I didn't suggest you did," she said gently.

"It was here when I first came to Nabby's," Denny said.

Will said, "I thought you hadn't known about it."

"I…We're not supposed to talk about it. We're s'posed to pretend it ain't there. When I first got here, I asked Johnny about it, and he punched me in the head and said it wasn't none of my business and to forget I seen it. *Saw* it."

Handing the lantern back to Denny, Will jumped down from the coal crib and pulled out a handkerchief to wipe the fine black dust off his hands.

"I'd like to have a look," Nell said, handing Will her shawl as she gathered up her skirts.

"Easy, there." Draping the shawl over his shoulder, Will took her hand to steady her as she stepped up onto the wooden divider, then wrapped his hands around her middle as she leaned over to look through the spy hole. So tightly corseted was she that his long fingers nearly spanned her waist.

Still unsteady in her fashionably dainty, spoon-heeled boots, Nell braced her hands on the wall to balance herself—or rather, her fingertips, since she didn't want to get her borrowed lace mitts too dirty. She closed one eye to focus in on the candlelit flat, of which she had an excellent view from above. The bed and the area to the side of it were completely visible. She couldn't help wondering if the couple who'd rumpled that quilt had been secretly observed as they'd disported themselves.

Would it have been Mary and Johnny on that bed, or Mary and a customer? Was Johnny doing the spying, or did other men pay to watch? Did Mary realize she was being spied upon, or had Johnny kept that fact from her? Nell imagined being watched unawares while she shared her bed with a man. The thought inspired a rush of humiliated outrage on Mary's behalf.

"I don't even want to know why this hole is here." Nell glanced down to find Will's gaze on her bosom, which was pretty much directly at the level of his eyes. With her leaning over as she was, and sporting such a deep décolletage, it must have been quite an eyeful.

He looked up at her, and abruptly away, with a discomfited, almost pained expression. Nell found her embarrassment outweighed by amusement that the urbane, unflappable William Hewitt should not only act like a "leering boor," but display such chagrin at being caught at it.

Keeping one hand on the wall for support, Nell lifted her skirts and prepared to step down.

"Careful." Still gripping her about the waist, Will lifted her as easily as if she were made of papier maché. He set her down gently, his hands seeming almost to caress her as he withdrew them.

Nell murmured her thanks without meeting his eyes, unaccountably rattled that he had the strength to handle her so effortlessly. He draped the shawl over her arms, offering not one word of protest this time when she pulled it up over her shoulders, tying it in front for good measure.

"Is this door always kept locked?" Will asked Denny.

"It is now. You got to get the key from Mother if you want to get in here—even Riley."

"Now?" Will asked. "It didn't used to be?"

"Um, no. Only about the past year or so. Before that, it didn't even have a lock on it."

"Why did Mother Nabby decide to lock it?" Will asked. "Had there been thefts?"

"Dunno. I guess. So, uh, you folks all done here, or…?"

Will said, "Yeah, I reckon we've seen all there is to see."

"How awful," Nell said as Denny locked the doors to the flat and the coal cellar, "a man getting murdered right in that very room. Were you here when it happened?" she asked him.

"Yeah. Well…Nobody knew what was happening downstairs, you know? It was Tuesday night, and Tuesday night's fight night. Tuesday and Saturday. It's godawful noisy on fight night, what with everybody screamin' and howlin' and carryin' on. It's louder even than right now, with them…with those can-can dancers."

"Who fought Tuesday night?" Will asked as they made their way back through the basement. Interesting; Nell wouldn't have thought to ask that.

Denny said, "First fight was Finn Cassidy against Davey Kerr. Second fight was Jimmy Muldoon against Phelix McCann. That was it, just the two fights."

"When did the murder happen?" Will asked.

"During the second fight, while Muldoon was fightin' McCann. They was…they were in the middle of the third round when Pru runs upstairs, screamin—"

"Pru?" Nell said.

"Pru Devine," Denny said as he hung the lantern back on its hook at the bottom of the stairs. "I think her real name is Prudence. She come runnin' upstairs screamin about a murder. 'Johnny Cassidy's been shot in the head.' She said the guy that done it was still down there, and he had a gun. Riley came runnin', and the girls, and Finn. Everybody came runnin'. The fight stopped. Mother made Riley lock the basement door, and she sent me out to fetch a cop. I found Constable Skinner down at the corner, and I brung him…brought him back and he took over and…" Denny shrugged. "He asked some questions, and they hauled the body away, and that was that."

"Who did he question, do you know?" Nell asked. *We got three witnesses that say he done it*, Skinner had claimed.

"Well, I know he talked to Pru, 'cause I guess she was the first one that saw what happened. She had a customer down here, and he came upstairs, too, but he slipped away in all the commotion before Skinner could talk to him. I reckon he didn't want to have to give his name to the cops and have everybody findin' out what he'd been doing down here with Pru."

"I reckon not," Will said with a little smile.

"Do you know whether Constable Skinner tried to track down this customer?" Nell asked.

"He said it wouldn't be necessary, 'cause it was clear as day what happened."

"Why open the door to other possibilities," Will said to Nell, "once he'd decided who to accuse?"

"Do you happen to know what Pru told Constable Skinner?" Nell asked Denny.

"Yeah, I heard she said Detective Cook killed Johnny. He's this state cop that comes around here sometimes. That's what she said, but…"

"But you don't believe he did it?" Nell asked.

"I know he didn't. He…he wouldn't. He just wouldn't, not him. He ain't like the blood tubs that hang around here. *Isn't.* He says the law is everything, it's how moral men keep the world safe for women and children, for the future. He says it's never right to break the law, 'cause it's like a pact among good people everywhere, and without it, there's no such thing as civilization."

"It sounds as if you're pretty friendly with Detective Cook," Nell said.

"We chew the fat sometimes, when he's around. He tries to make me talk like a highbrow, 'cause he says folks judge you mostly by what comes out of your mouth, so if you want to get ahead in life, you have to talk like the person you want to be. He says you gotta think about where you're goin', not where you've been."

"That's very true," said Nell, who had been blessed enough to have effected just such a transformation herself.

"He brings me newspapers to read," Denny said, "and copies of *Harper's* and *Putnam's* and other magazines when he's done with 'em, and books from the liberry. He brung me this one… *brought* me this one." He pulled out the book that he'd tucked in his trousers and showed it to them.

"*The Last of the Mohicans,*" Will said. "Great story."

"It's pretty good," Denny said as he tucked it back in. "Mary liked it a lot. I used to lend her my books to read on the sly. Johnny didn't like her reading 'cause he said it made her look like a bluestocking and gave her ideas, but really I think it was 'cause he couldn't read so well himself—not well enough to read a book, anyways. My favorite book is *Ivanhoe.* I read that one a second time after Mary was done with it, or almost. I had to give it back before I was finished so Detective Cook could return it to the liberry."

"I could buy you a copy," Will said, "and then you could read it as often as you—"

"No. Uh-uh. Thanks all the same, mister. Detective Cook said the same thing, but that's different than gettin' it from the liberry. That'd be like a hand-out. He's offered me money, too, Detective Cook, but I wouldn't take that, neither. Either."

"Self-reliance is an admirable trait," Nell said, "but it makes people feel good to help people they like."

"My mum said never to take any hand-outs, and I don't mean to start now, just 'cause she ain't here to see it. I told that to Detective Cook, and he said then I better plan on lots of hard work, on account of that's what it takes to get ahead with no help from anybody else, so that's what I aim to do."

Will said, "If Detective Cook is the top-notch fella you make him out to be, I can understand why you don't think he killed Johnny Cassidy. But then, why do you reckon this Pru said he did?"

With a look of disgust, Denny said, "She says she seen him standin' over Johnny's body with his gun drawn, but—"

"'Cause that's what I seen, you little pimple." One of the red curtains whipped open, revealing a dark-haired young woman in tawdry finery, hooking up her bodice. She had pallid skin, sullen, black-limned eyes, and the kind of squashy lips that always look freshly punched. The furnishings in the "dance booth" consisted of a blanket-covered pallet on the floor and a straight-backed chair, on which sat an obese, mustachioed gentleman in his shirt-sleeves, grunting with effort as he squeezed his silk-stockinged foot into a shoe.

"You callin' me a liar?" Pru asked Denny as she sauntered toward them, hands on hips, the top few hooks of her bodice still undone. She brought with her a sweetly sour tang of sweat and rose oil.

"Were you even sober enough that night to know what you seen?" Denny demanded, standing his own.

"Since us girls ain't allowed to drink on the job," she sneered, "I reckon I musta been."

Denny said, "Aw, c'mon, Pru, I ain't blind and deaf, and I got a nose on me. Most of the time, when you show up here, you're half-soused already. I've seen you sneakin' sips from the customers' drinks, and I've heard you beggin' Riley for 'just a little taste just to get you through the night.' You were prob'ly too corned that night to know what you seen, and now—"

"Yeah, well, just so happens I was as sober that night as I am right now, worse luck, and I know damn well what I seen. I seen Johnny Cassidy layin' there in a pool of blood, and that big black Irish cop standin' over him with his gun in his hand."

Her customer, upon hearing this, glanced curiously in their direction as he shrugged his braces over his shoulders.

"Did you hear the gunshot?" Will asked her. "Was that what drew you to the flat?"

Pru's gaze lit on Will and lingered there for a moment, a spark igniting in her flat black eyes. She sized Nell up swiftly, head to toe, then turned back to Will. Reaching into a pocket of her skirt, she produced a little tarnished brass compact and flipped it open. "Who's askin'?"

"My name's Tom Dougherty," Will said, "I need to rent a room, and I'm lookin' at this one, but to be honest, the notion of some loco running around shooting people in the head makes me think maybe I should be lookin' someplace else. *She* likes the place—" he cocked his head toward Nell "—but I ain't so sure. I got some questions I'd like answered first."

"You two hitched?" Pru asked.

Nell was about to answer yes, having agreed with Will that they would pose as Jack Dougherty and his wife, Moira, when Will said, "Nah. Moira, here, she's one of the girls I…take care of." He gave Pru a slippery grin Nell had never seen before and hoped to never see again.

Pru smiled knowingly as she dabbed up a fingertip of crimson lip rouge and slicked it over her lips, her gaze never leaving Will's. She rubbed her lips together, snicked the compact shut, and said, "I heard a bang from that direction, but I wasn't real sure what it was. There was a fight goin' on right over our heads that night, and it was even louder than when them can-can dancers is goin' at it, like now. I finished up with my john and went over to the flat to check it out. The door was open, and that's when I seen what I seen."

"Detective Cook standing over the body with a gun."

"It was *his* gun," Pru said. "His coat was hangin' open, like, and I seen his holster, and it was empty."

"That still doesn't mean he done it," Denny said.

"You wasn't even there, you little gnat," Pru said. "If you'd seen him standin' there with that gun, lookin' all grim and mean, you'd of known he done it. I screamed so loud my throat was sore till the next day. I thought for sure he was gonna aim that gun at me and pull the trigger."

"Did you see Mary Molloy?" Will asked her.

"Yeah, she was there. She had this old satchel layin' open on the bed, and she was throwin' her clothes into it without even foldin' 'em, just kind of shovin' 'em in there, all frantic like. There was blood drippin' outa her nose, and she didn't even stop to wipe it off. It got on some of the clothes."

"Blood?" Will said.

"She'd taken a few licks," Pru said nonchalantly. "One side of her face was all beat up, but it wasn't the first time. You'd see bruises on her sometimes, under the makeup. That's the kind she was, always askin' for it."

"She wasn't, neither!" Denny exclaimed.

"What would *you* know about it?" Pru shot back. "You ain't even had a girl yet, much less tried to rein in a load of mischief like Mary Molloy."

"She wasn't a load of mischef," Denny said. "She didn't swear and smoke and give herself cheap. She wasn't anything like the rest of you blowers."

"She was a damn sight worse, if you ask me," Pru countered, "slippin' 'round on Johnny like an alleycat. Johnny did what he had to do to keep her in line—not that it did any good. If she was the kind to learn her lesson, she never would of taken up with Cook."

"You don't know that," Denny said.

"You think the two of them were involved?" Will asked Pru. "Detective Cook and Mary Molloy?"

"I know they were." Pru reached up to tidy her unkempt top-knot, arching her back so as to display her charms to Will in a way that Nell found crudely obvious. "Everybody knew, or at least had their suspicions. Then, one night about a week ago, I seen him leavin' their flat through the basement door, the one that lets out onto the backyard. He looked all around while he was comin' up the stairs, like to make sure there weren't nobody nearby to see him."

"How did *you* manage to see him, then?" Will asked.

"I was comin' back from the chicken house. He didn't see me, though. I hid behind the privy till he was gone."

"The chicken house?" Will said. "Ain't that were Finn Cassidy lives?"

"She's sweet on Finn, ain't you, Pru?" Denny said. "She thinks if she gives it to him for free, he'll turn sweet on *her*, but all he wants from her is a quick—"

"Go to hell and help your mother make bitch pie, you mangy little fly-blow," Pru spat out.

Denny said, "It's true. She moons over him like he's the Prince of Wales, and he just uses her for what she's good at. It ain't her he likes. It's—"

"Denny!" boomed a voice from the top of the stairs: Riley, the bartender. "Get your bony little arse up here with that Jameson's."

Denny hesitated, his jaw set.

"Better hurry along, Denny-boy," Pru taunted in a sing-songy voice. "Your master's callin' you."

"Now," Riley bellowed.

The boy shot Pru a look of loathing. "If you want the flat, you'll have to go talk to Mother," he told Will, and sprinted up the stairs with the jug. Pru stuck her tongue out at his retreating back.

"So, you were able to watch Cook from where you were hiding?" Will asked her.

"Yeah, he got halfway up the stairs, when Mary comes out and says, 'Hey, didn't you forget somethin'?' He says, 'Oh, yeah, sorry, slipped my mind,' and pulls some greenbacks outa his pockets and gives 'em to her."

"You're sure it was money he gave her?" Will asked. "You said it was nighttime. It musta been dark."

"She was carryin' a lamp. I seen it real clear. Mary stuffs the money down her top and says somethin' like, 'What if Johnny finds out?' or 'I'm worried he's gonna find out,' or somethin' like that, and Cook kinda strokes her hair and says 'He ain't gonna find out so long as we're careful.'"

"Why should she have been worried about Johnny finding out?" Will asked. "I mean, she *was* hooking, right?"

"Sure, but she specialized. Only the live ones for her—them with the deepest pockets. If she caught the eye of some regular fella, some sailor or dockworker or such, she'd give 'em the cold shoulder. But if he was dressed all fine, with a good coat and a fancy walkin' stick, she'd giggle and coo and let him take her downstairs."

"Did Johnny pimp for her?"

"Well, she reeled in the johns all by herself. He didn't go out and find 'em, or anything like that. Most nights, she'd be just sittin' there at one of the tables, drinkin' her milk, and—"

"Milk?" Will said.

"She looks younger than she is, lots younger, and Johnny liked her to play that up. I think she's about my age, early twenties, but she's real small and slender, with them big blue eyes. You'd take her for maybe thirteen if you seen her sittin' there with her milk and her braids and them white collars and cuffs. If some rich snoot took an interest, she'd let him take her downstairs. Then, about a minute or two later, Johnny would head back that way, so I reckon he was following 'em down there. Waitin' 'round for the money, prob'ly. Maybe makin' sure she gave it all to him. Or maybe he made the john pay him directly. I heard he just doled out a half-bit to her from time to time, and she had to beg him for that much."

"Cook may not have been rich," Will said, "but if he was a paying customer, why should Johnny have had a problem with it? Why should Mary have felt like she had to keep it a secret from him?"

Perhaps, Nell thought, because he didn't get to watch.

Pru shrugged as she slid hairpins out of the topknot and pushed them back in. "Maybe Mary wanted to keep Cook's money all to herself 'stead of handin' it over to Johnny. Or maybe it was 'cause her and Cook had a little bit more goin' on between 'em than just business. She didn't have no other reg'lars. He was the only one I know of that ever came back for seconds, and when I was watchin' 'em that time, well…He didn't look at her like she was no whore, and he didn't talk to her like the johns talk to the rest of us. He was…gentle like."

"He paid her, though," Will said.

"That don't mean he didn't have them kinds of feelings for her. Didn't you ever give money to some girl you fancied? Or special little gifts, even if you knew she'd just turn around and pawn 'em?"

Will conceded her point with a little duck of his head and a rueful smile.

"Thing is," Pru said, "only fella Mary Molloy was s'posed to be spreadin' them skinny little legs for on a reg'lar basis was Johnny Cassidy. If he'd of found out about Cook, he'd of likely wrung her neck."

Will said, "You told Constable Skinner all this, about Cook leaving Mary's place that night?"

"He asked me if I'd ever seen Cook doin' anything untoward. That was how he put it—'untoward.' So I told him about Cook and Mary."

"Did anyone else know?" he asked. "Had you told anyone, after you saw Cook leave her flat that night?"

"Not right after, but I thought about it. I never did like Mary. Uppity little bitch, thinks she's better'n the rest of us working birds."

"If you didn't like her," Will asked, "how come you didn't tell?"

With a sly little smile, Pru said, "I had my reasons."

"You decided to blackmail her, didn't you?" Nell asked.

It was the first time Nell had spoken, and it was probably a bad idea, because Pru cut her a scornful look and said, "I reckon I'd best be gettin' back upstairs before Mother starts wonderin' what's takin' me so long. She don't like us girls to spend too much time down here. Eats into her profits as well as ours."

"She takes a cut of what you're paid?" Will asked.

"She takes the money and give us *our* cut, which is half of what the johns pay—greedy old haybag."

"Don't seem quite fair," Will said.

"It's that or the street," Pru said. "Used to be, it was the other way 'round—they'd pay us, and we'd give Mother her half—but Mother always thought we was cheatin' her. Like, if we told her we just did a French trick, she'd say no you didn't, it took too long, it must been reg'lar, and she'd keep it all, on account of reg'lar costs double what French does."

"In that case," Will said, "you must have been tempted to get away with what you could from time to time. I know *I* would have been."

"From time to time," Pru admitted. "Not too often, 'cause we didn't want to push our luck. One time, 'bout four, five years ago—" she glanced up the stairs and lowered her voice "—this girl Ellie was holdin' back way too much. She got careless, you know? Well, Mother found out, and next thing you know, they find Ellie floatin' facedown in the Charles River. Coroner said she'd been strangled and dumped there. After that, we toed the line, you know what I mean? When Mother started doin' the collectin' herself, I was actually relieved."

"Understandable," Will said. "I've just got one more question, if you don't mind."

"You sure got a lot of 'em."

"Like I said, I just want to know what really happened before I lay down my money for that flat."

"I told you what happened."

"Did anybody else see what you saw?" Will asked. "Seems to me I heard there were other witnesses."

"Yeah, there was a couple of young swells smoking gong back in there." She nodded toward the hop joint. "They came stumblin' out when they heard me scream, and they seen Cook standin' over Johnny with that gun. They were hopped up pretty bad. One of 'em had to hold onto the wall just so's he could stand. The other one actually started gigglin', like it was funny or somethin'. I high-tailed it upstairs, but I think them two mighta just gone and laid back down and smoked some more dope, 'cause I didn't see 'em after that."

"Did you recognize them?" Will asked.

"I never seen 'em here before. I think they was just a couple of young fellas from Beacon Hill or the Back Bay out for a little taste of the lowlife. A little night spree in the North End, you know?"

"Do you know whether the constable who came questioned them?"

"I dunno, but if he did, I reckon they woulda told him the same thing I did. Don't listen to that stupid Denny Delaney. He just don't want to face up to his precious Detective Cook doin' somethin' like that, but I seen what I seen, and I know what I know. You ask me, Cook was drillin' Mary, and Johnny came in and caught 'em. Johnny gets worked up, so Cook shoots him in the head and runs off with Mary."

"Any idea where they might have gone?" Will asked.

"I don't know, and I don't care, but if she knows what's good for her, she'll stay clear of here. Finn says she's the reason his brother got killed. He says he'll put a bullet in *her* brain if she ever shows her face here again."

CHAPTER TEN

NELL AND WILL STOOD IN the doorway of Mother Nabby's back room listening to Finn Cassidy, looming over her desk with his back to them, make his case for not renting out his late brother's flat.

"Christ Amighty, Mother, it's only been two days since Johnny got killed," Finn said heatedly. "It ain't right, lettin' somebody else move in so soon."

"He ain't comin' back, y'know," Mother said around a mouthful of the roasted leg of lamb sitting on a platter in front of her.

"I know he ain't—"

"And meantime, I got a business to run." She washed down the lamb with a long swallow of beer, eyeing Nell and Will over the rim of the tankard. "Well?" she said as she wiped her mouth with the back of her bare arm. "D'you want the place or not?"

"I think so, but I have a few questions," Will said as he ushered Nell into the room with a hand on her back. He kept it there, for which she was grateful. Mother Nabby made her nervous, and it was comforting, that physical contact.

"Johnny paid you through the end of the month," Finn told Mother, "so you got no right to rent it out till August."

Mother slammed the tankard down so hard that beer sloshed out onto her desk, but if she noticed, she didn't seem to care. "You tellin' me what I got a *right* to do in my own place, Finn Cassidy?" she demanded, a forbidding glint in those hard little raisin eyes.

He actually cringed, raising his hands in a placating gesture. "It's just…you already been paid, so—"

"I been paid the rent," she said, "but I ain't been paid the rest of what I'm due."

"He always gave you your cut of what Mary took in," Finn said.

"Not all of it, and don't you try and deny it. Plus, he was skimmin' part of the take from the other, always did."

"You don't know that."

"I can't prove it, but I know it. You spend enough years doin' business with ragsters like him, you learn to tell when they're dealin' you dirty. Plus, half the time he was doin' bouncer duty, he was so drunk, *he* the one pickin' the fights. I needed a bouncer to bounce *him*."

"Um, Miss Nabby?"

They turned to find Pru's portly customer, now smartly turned out in a frock coat and silk cravat, standing in the doorway, top hat in one hand, gloves in the other.

"Evenin', Mr. Jones," Mother said. "You were with Pru, right? That'll be eight dollars. You can pay Riley at the bar."

"I, er...was wondering if you wouldn't be so kind as to start an account for me," he said.

"C'mon in, then." Wiping her greasy hands on a napkin, Mother withdrew a small, leatherbound book from a pocket of her pinafore, dipped a steel pen into her inkwell, and made a notation in the ledger. From where Nell was standing, she could read it upside down.

July 7, 1870
Josiah Honeycutt
Regular w/Pru
$8.00

Nell recognized the name. Josiah Honeycutt sat on the Boston City Council.

"If I could just have your signature right here, Mr. Jones." Mother handed the pen to "Mr. Jones," who signed the ledger and departed.

"You let the johns pay with credit?" Will asked as Mother returned the little book to the pocket.

"For them that deserve it, them I can trust. 'Specially if they're rich and well-connected, 'cause then chances are they won't try and wriggle out of payin' up when the time comes. They know what I can do to them if I set my mind to it." She pinched up some tobacco from a Black Cat tin on her desk and stuffed it into her pipe.

"Allow me," Will said as he leaned over to light the pipe, all smiles and gallantry.

Mother surveyed him coolly as he did so. The front of her pinafore, over the mountain of her breasts, bore spatters of grease and beer, as well as little flecks of lamb that hadn't made it into her mouth.

"So the flat will serve?" she asked, expanding her gaze to encompass Nell.

"I expect so," Will said as he flicked out the match. "Mind you, the blood's a bit much."

"I'll have that scrubbed up," Mother said. "When are you fixin' on movin' in?"

"Not for a few days," Will said.

"It'll be gone by then. You'll never know it was there."

"Is it true the former tenant was murdered?" Nell asked.

"By a cop," Finn growled, "over the rotten little grubber he was livin' with."

"Grubber?" Mother said with a smirky little smile. "C'mon, Finn, I seen the way you'd look at her when yer brother wasn't watchin'."

"There ain't a man in this place didn't look at her that way," Finn said, his face darkening. "Her in them little schoolgirl frocks, battin' them big cow eyes at everything in trousers."

Mother said, "Funny, I don't seem to recall her battin' them at your particular trousers."

"She's a lyin', stinkin' little scut," he railed, spittle flying. "She got my brother killed 'cause she was grindin' some cop, fer Chrissakes, and you don't even care."

"That's enough, Finn," Mother said in a low, ominous tone.

"Johnny got shot in the head over that little bitch, and you just sit here like some prize sow, seein' how much money you can squeeze outa his—"

"Riley!" she bellowed.

The bartender came runnin. "Yes, ma'am."

"Our friend here ain't thinkin' too straight," Mother said without wresting her malevolent gaze from Finn, "He's sayin' some things that make me think he ain't right in the head. Why don't you take him out back to the chicken house 'fore he ends up hurt?"

There was a subtle emphasis on that last part about ending up hurt, very subtle, but from the way the color leached from Riley's face, it was clear that Mother's implicit threat wasn't lost on him. For a bruiser like Finn Cassidy to fear a woman spoke volumes about Mother Nabby's ability to punish those who displeased her. No doubt the doomed Ellie wasn't the first or last victim of her appetite for revenge.

"C'mon, pal," Riley said, and pulled Finn out of the room by his shirtsleeve. "Lay down and get some sleep, and when you wake up tomorrow, try and not be such a horse's arse."

"Is it true Mary Molloy was killed over a cop?" Nell asked.

"She was bangin' him, I know *that*," Mother said as she tore a shred of lamb off the leg with her fingers and crammed it into her mouth. "State cop, big mick that comes around here from time to time to try and keep us on the up and up. He'd sneak into the basement flat through the outside stairs when Johnny wasn't around."

"You know this for a fact?" Nell asked.

"Little birdie told me, so I had Riley bring him to me—the cop. He admitted it, said he was kinda like keepin' her, but he didn't want Johnny to find out 'less he take it out on Mary, and of course he didn't want his wife findin' out, neither. I'll say this for him, he knew enough to grease my palm without me needin' to spell it out. I told him just nail Mary on the sly and make sure he didn't get caught, 'cause I didn't need any trouble with Johnny. So then, don't you know he gets sloppy and lets Johnny find him bouncin' her in his own bed. Stupid goddamn mutton-shunter."

"So you think that's the way it really happened?" Will asked.

"I don't know how it happened," Mother said, taking a puff on her pipe as she ripped off another hunk of lamp. "You ask me, that's more'n likely how it went. What's it to you, anyway?"

"I'm asking 'cause I'm little worried about Moira's safety," he said, pulling Nell close to him. Her arm ended up crushed awkwardly between them, so she curled it around his waist, hoping it looked more natural than it felt. Absurdly, she felt the blood rise in her cheeks.

Will said, "If shootings are a regular thing around here—"

"They ain't, and they better not get to be," Mother said. "I pay four-hundred and fifty bucks a week in protection to keep things nice and quiet here."

"Yeah, well, things weren't too quiet Tuesday night," Will pointed out. "Are you sure the people you're paying are doing their job?"

Mother sat back heavily in her thronelike chair, chewing as she raised the pipe to her mouth. "Three-hundred of it gets divided amongst the cops at the Division Eight station house over on Commercial and Salutation. Most of the local joints pay 'em—the ones with card games or whores, anyway—but we pay the most, 'cause we got that plus the gong, plus the wagering on the fights.

Little rat called Skinner makes the rounds all over this neighborhood every Saturday night. Strolls up and down North Street, his pockets gettin' fatter n' fatter. If he wasn't a gun-totin' bluebottle, he wouldn't make it half a block around here with that much dough on him. The only cop that ever really hangs around here is that state cop that was screwin' Mary. He'd come and sit down like a regular customer, drink himself some cider, walk around and talk to folks…So far he ain't arrested nobody, so who knows—even though he answers to the state, maybe he's pocketing part of Skinner's take."

"The payoffs are so they'll turn a blind eye to what goes on here?" Nell asked.

"And so's they'll come runnin' when I send for 'em. If a fight breaks out, and it's a bad one with a roomful of drunks raisin' hell, it sometimes take more than one or two bouncers to make it stop—that, and it doesn't hurt to let them that was in on it spend the night in lockup."

"What about the other hundred and fifty?" Will asked. "Who gets that?"

"That goes to Brian O'Donagh. You know him?"

"I know *of* him," Will said. "The Sons of Eire."

"They help out when the problem has to do with things the cops have to pretend they don't know about. Like they make sure them that cheat at cards or take knives to the girls never show up here again."

"And how do they manage that?" Will asked.

Mother answered that with a how-do-you-think look. "Let's just say I don't ask. O'Donagh also makes sure his own boys leave us be. Enough jawin'. You want the flat or not?"

"How much?" Will asked.

"Depends. You want it for business or just to live in, or both?"

"Both, I guess. Moira will be living there," he said as he stroked her side, "and she'll also be conducting some business."

"It's forty a week, plus six bucks for every ten she takes in."

"Six?" Nell said. "I heard the other girls only pay you half."

"Those girls are *my* girls," Mother said. "I got an investment in them. Every john you take away from them is one my girls don't get, and there's just so many of them to go around. Sixty percent. Take it or leave it."

"Was that your agreement with Johnny and Mary? Sixty percent?" Nell noticed, in the corner of her eye, Will smiling at the way she was dickering over the cut.

"Mary wasn't a sporting girl," Mother said.

"She wasn't…?" Nell began. "But I thought…"

"Not in the usual way," Mother amended. "My arrangement with Johnny was a little more complicated, but he still owed me a cut—not that I always got what was due me. Johnny held out." Turning to Will with a frosty glint in her eye, Mother said, "Don't hold out."

Mother sent Will out to the bar to pay the first month's rent to Riley, who handled her cash transactions, but she asked Nell to stay behind for a minute so that they could "get to know each other."

As soon as Will was out of earshot, Mother said, "Why are you here?"

"I'm sorry?"

"I mean what the hell is a pretty little jay like you doin' in a rumhole like this, when you could be hawkin' your mutton in some highfalutin flash house over on Cambridge Street?"

"Um…"

"Look at you," Mother said, gesturing with a colossal pudding arm. "You got class. You can't hide class, no matter how much tit you show. And there's somethin' in your eyes, an innocence, a sweetness. You blush real good. Johns'll pay top dollar for them blushes. Maidenheads is big business in your line of work."

"I haven't had one of those since I was sixteen," Nell said truthfully; not since her wedding night with Duncan.

"Fakin' it is easier than you think. I can give you a few point-ers, and I'll tell you, men believe what they want to believe. You could easily pass for cherry—time and again."

It occurred to Nell that Mother Nabby was, for whatever rea-son, trying very hard to talk Nell into this. Plumbing her mind for a reason to put her off, Nell said, "If I work at a regular brothel, I'll have to pay the proprietress, and—"

"You'll be payin' *me* if you work out of here," Mother said. "And him, too." She glanced at the door through which Will had departed. "He's mackin' for you, ain't he? What'll be left for you? Ten percent? Twenty? At a first class bumshop, you'll be chargin' more and keepin' more."

"Um, I'll...I guess I'll think about it. But, um, in the meantime—"

"You let me know, and I'll find you a place. I know a few madams that run very discreet houses, very high-tone and dis-criminating. Only the best johns. Clean, rich. They tip pretty heavy, some of 'em."

"Pardon me for asking," Nell said, "but what's in it for you?"

"They'll pay me for findin' you, and believe me, it'll be a lot more than what I'll make off my cut of your takings here. Mind you, you won't owe me one red cent. It'll all come out of their pocket."

"I'll, um, take it under advisement," Nell said.

"You do that. Meanwhile..." Mother shifted in her chair, looking off toward the bar. "You want to go out there and fetch me Flora, or one of them other girls? I need the jakes, and I got trouble walkin' on account of my gout."

"Oh. Um...I can take you out back," Nell offered.

"Out back?" Mother snorted in derision. "Honey, I don't pee in no damn outhouse. I got my own personal W.C. right over there." She nodded toward a door in the back of the room. "Hand me those, would you?" She pointed to a pair of canes leaning against the wall.

Nell brought them to her and supported her while she heaved herself with a groan of effort out of the chair, one hand gripping the head of each wobbly cane. Mother's skin felt unctuously soft, and moist where it was bare. She smelled, through the haze of tobacco and lamb grease, like something old and stale and sick. Standing, she looked even more massive, a good five-hundred pounds if she was an ounce.

Walking was an arduous ordeal for Mother Nabby. For each footstep, she had to plant the cane, shuffle a foot, and regain her precarious balance. Nell drew upon her years of nursing to assist Mother without displaying any hint of impatience or distaste.

"I was right about you," Mother grunted as she huffed and puffed her way across the floor. "You're just naturally sweet, ain't you? I'm tellin' you, you can get top dollar for that. Top dollar."

CHAPTER ELEVEN

B Y THE TIME NELL FINISHED escorting Mother Nabby to and from the W.C. and made it out front to the bar, Will was deep in conversation with Pru at a dark little corner table. A waiter girl set two fresh drinks in front of them and removed two empty glasses. As soon as she turned away, Will switched the two glasses, exchanging his drink for Pru's, which presumably contained no alcohol. They shared a conspiratorial smile that made the hairs on Nell's nape prickle, and then Pru, sitting with her back mostly turned toward Nell, lifted her glass and gulped down a good portion of it.

She said something to Will, to which he replied—his lips were easy enough to read—"You're welcome." Leaning over the little table, Pru trailed a hand along the lapel of his sack coat while saying something that made Will smile. She might have been sweet on Finn, as Denny Delaney claimed, but it would appear that didn't prevent her from testing the waters elsewhere.

As he sat back to lift his drink, Will caught sight of Nell and tilted his head in a discreet beckoning gesture. The raucous conversation in the bar, on top of the din from the music hall—the can-can dancers were still stomping and kicking—made it impossible to hear anything of Will and Pru's conversation until she was almost upon them.

"...wondering why you didn't tell anybody about seeing Detective Cook leaving Mary's flat that night," Will was saying.

"I just figgered it'd be smarter to tell Mary what I knew, and see what it was worth to her for me to keep my mouth shut." Pru's speech was a little woolly around the edges. The booze was relaxing her, as Will had no doubt hoped it would.

"That *was* smart," Will said.

"Ten bucks a week, and she didn't even try to bargain me down. She was scared Johnny would find out. He had a temper, just like his brother. My pa was like that, and my uncles. Comes with the territory, I reckon. You want a real man, not some namby-pamby, you gotta be ready to take the bad with the good. Course, I only got the one payment from her 'fore she up and left, but at least I'm ten dollars richer than I woulda been."

"Tom—here you are," Nell said as she joined them. "I've been looking for you."

"Moira." Will rose and pulled out a chair for her. Pru slid her a look that dripped poison as she pulled a booklet of rolling papers and a little tobacco pouch from the chatelaine on her belt.

"Have one of mine," Will said, opening his tin of Turkish Orientals and offering it to her.

"Oh, Tommy, you're a reg'lar gentleman, ain't you?" Pru said as she took a cigarette.

Tommy? Nell darted an oh-brother look toward Will, who appeared to be biting his lip.

"I ain't never smoked an already-rolled cigarette," Pru said as Will lit it for her.

"They may be a little stale," Will said. "I don't smoke very much anymore."

"Tastes like heaven to me, but then I reckon I'm easy," the whore purred, her gaze locked on Will's.

"So, do you think Detective Cook and Mary were in love?" Will asked Pru.

She shook her head as she drew on the cigarette. "If he was, he wouldn't of shared her. Men ain't generous like that with women they're serious about. They like to keep 'em all to themselves. Me,

I figger if a fellas's got an appetite, there should be more'n enough to go 'round."

"I shouldn't think Cook had too much choice about sharing Mary," Will said, "considering what she did for a living." He was getting tired, it seemed to Nell; his natural British inflection was starting to creep back into his voice. Or perhaps he just reasoned that Pru was too tipsy at this point to notice or care.

"I'm not talkin' about her johns," Pru said. "I'm talkin' about this fella Cook brung around a few days ago, Monday, I think. Yeah, Monday night—pretty early, 'round eight or nine, 'cause it was just gettin' dark. Some pal of his, a timber-toe."

"Timber-toe?" Nell said.

"He had a wooden leg. I think he mighta had a glass eye, too. Pretty normal looking other than that, real nice clothes, but gammy nonetheless."

Will met Nell's gaze. *Ebenezer Shute.*

"Are you saying Cook brought him here to…share Mary with him?" Nell asked.

"That was my take on it. The two of them was sitting up front near the bar, drinkin'. Well, Timber-toe was drinkin'—pretty heavy, too. Not Cook. I ain't never seen him lift a glass here. Mary was sittin' in her corner with her milk. She didn't so much as look in their direction, prob'ly 'cause Johnny was prowlin' 'round, and she didn't want him to see her and Cook bein' too friendly. They was lookin' at her, though—Cook and the crip—and talkin' 'bout her."

"How could you be sure of that?" Nell asked.

"I passed by their table a couple times. I heard Cook sayin', 'Her name's Mary Molloy,' and that she was older than she looked, and 'a real good sort.' Later, when I passed by again, the crip's sayin' how beautiful she is, and how he's got to have her—which just goes to show you that crips'll settle for anything, 'cause she's got the puniest little diddies I ever seen on a grown woman."

"Did he take her downstairs?" Will asked.

"Not right then. Cook asked Riley, the bartender, where's the cleanest place to get oysters nearby, and they left. Then, a couple hours later, Timber-toe comes back alone, walks right up to Mary's table—none too steady, I could tell he was fuddled—and sets himself down. Ten minutes later, she's sashayin' down to the basement with him stumblin' along behind her on that wooden leg."

"Did Johnny follow them downstairs?" Nell asked.

"Sure, he always did. 'Bout twenty minutes later, him and the crip are back up here, with Johnny kinda shovin' the crip toward the front door, and the crip shovin' back and yellin' 'bout how he wasn't gonna take it, how he knew what was Johnny was up to, that kinda thing. He got even more worked up when Johnny got Finn to help muscle him out of the building. He's yellin', 'You'll be sorry, I'll make you sorry, just see if I don't.' That kind of thing. He fell down when Johnny pushed him out onto the sidewalk, on account of the wooden leg—and him bein' so soused, I guess. There was a big crowd out there, and they all laughed and kind of, you know, made fun of him."

Nell looked toward Will, who was sitting in a pensive posture, arms folded, one hand covering his mouth. He met Nell's gaze and raised his eyebrows.

Pru chuckled at the memory. "He's screamin', 'I'll kill you, you bastard, you're a dead man,' with Johnny and Finn grinnin' and walkin' away, brushin' off their hands."

"Did you tell Constable Skinner about this incident?" Will asked.

"Nah," Pru said. "I tried to, but he kept goin' back to Cook, so I just figgered he didn't want to hear it."

Because, of course, he'd already homed in on Colin Cook as the man he intended to arrest for Johnny Cassidy's murder.

"May I ask you something, Pru?" Nell said.

Pru blew a stream of gin-scented smoke in Nell's face and formed her bloodred lips into a smile.

"We found a hole in a wall of the flat," Nell said, "the one between that room and the coal cellar."

"This is a rundown old building." Pru finished the rest of her drink in one breathless swallow, whereupon Will signaled for another round. "It's fallin' apart little by little, 'specially the basement. If you want a nice, fancy place with flowered wallpaper and Oriental carpets, you're gonna end up payin' a hell of a lot more than Mother'll charge you."

"It's not that kind of hole," Nell said. "Somebody made it deliberately, so they could spy on the flat from the coal cellar."

"I'll be damned," Pru said with a snorty little chuckle. "A spy hole. Some joints have 'em—you know, the kind of grinding shops where a fella can get anything he wants, long as he's got the green to pay for it? There's some johns like to watch other johns while they're peggin' the girls. Some of 'em, that's all they want to do, is just watch." She spat a fleck of tobacco onto the floor. "Their money."

No sooner were the fresh drinks delivered, and duly switched by Will, than Pru set about draining hers. "That hits the spot, Tommy," she sighed as she slumped back in her chair. "You're a real sport."

"So you didn't know anything about the hole downstairs?" Nell asked.

"Not till now. If I had to guess, I'd say Johnny was caterin' to them that likes to watch. He had more ways to make a dime than anybody I ever met—'cept maybe Mother. Course, after Mother locked the door to the coal cellar, he woulda had to get the key from her every time he wanted to..." Pru had been raising the cigarette to her mouth, but now she lowered it slowly. *"That's* why Mother put the lock on that door."

Nell and Will exchanged a look of bafflement. "Why?" Will asked.

"'Cause of Denny." Pru sat forward on her elbows, drink in one hand, cigarette in the other. "See, about a year ago, Denny got caught spyin' on Mary."

"Wait," Nell said. *"Spying?"*

"Watchin' her, you know, in her room in the basement. Prob'ly tryin' to catch her out of that little schoolgirl frock. He's been moonin' over her ever since his voice started crackin'. I didn't think about it much. I guess I thought he was peekin' in the window, or the door was half open or somethin'. But now I'm thinkin' he was lookin' at her through that spy hole you're talkin' about. On account of the coal cellar wasn't locked then. Anyway, they figgered it wasn't the first time he done it."

Will said, "'They,' being…"

Pru shrugged as she sucked on the cigarette. "Johnny, Mother, Riley…What I heard was Denny was peekin' in on Mary when Johnny came in and started workin' her over a little. So Denny barges into the room like the knight on the white horse. Little boneyard somehow manages to pull Johnny off her. Didn't hurt that Johnny was drunk as an owl. Mary runs off, Denny runs off, and Johnny passes out, on account of he's lushy. Anyway, the next day, Mother figgered Denny needed to be taught a lesson, so she sicced Finn on him."

"'Sicced?'" Nell wasn't sure she wanted to hear the rest of this.

"Denny's scared to death of Finn. Everybody is."

Nell said, "Yes, but Johnny was the…Well, if there was a victim in all this, it would have been Mary, but Johnny would be the natural choice to take revenge, wouldn't he?"

Pru said, "Yeah, but Finn is Johnny's brother, and a he's lot bigger than Johnny, to boot. He's a lot bigger than anybody, and once, a couple years ago…" Pru looked back and forth between

Nell and Will, smiling as if she were about to impart a delicious bit of news. "He killed a man in the ring."

"During a boxing match?" Will said. *"Killed* him?"

"Dead. Seven hammer-punches to the head, one after th'other, first round," Pru said proudly. "And he's come close a few other times, on account of he keeps whalin' even after they're down, that's how excited he gets. One fella, Johnny kicked him in the head, and after he came to, he went simple, has been ever since. They had to put him in the loony house. So anyways, Denny gets the shakes every time Finn comes near. Little priss."

The air left Nell's lungs. She heard it leave Will's.

"I was there when Finn cornered Denny," Pru said as she flicked her ash on the floor. "Little mollycoddle wet his pants. You could see it, this dark stain spreadin' down the front of his trousers. I just about laughed myself sick."

Nell glanced at Will. His jaw was thrust forward the way it got when he was holding himself back. His face looked as if it were carved of stone.

"Anyways," Pru said as she lifted her glass of gin, "Finn punched him in the stomach and the nose, and once he was on the ground, he stomped on his hand just for good measure. Went easy on him, if you ask me. Mother told him if she ever caught him spyin' on Mary again, or any of the other girls, she'd send him to Deer Island. And she put that padlock on the door to the coal cellar, just to keep him honest."

Pru dropped her cigarette butt on the floor and crushed it under her shoe.

"Do you suppose Denny made the hole or found it there?" Will asked Nell. "He told us it was there when he came to Nabby's, but he might have just been saying that."

"What *I'm* wondering," said Nell, "is why Mother padlocked the door, but didn't have the hole filled in. Regardless of whether

Denny made it or just stumbled on it, there was evidently some reason to keep it there, behind lock and key."

"Some reason that didn't have anything to do with Denny," Will said. "Someone wanted that hole for his own use."

"Johnny," Pru said, as if it were obvious. "So he could charge fellas to peek at Mary with those la-di-dah johns of hers."

"Or so he could peek at her himself," Nell said.

"What kind of a man was Johnny?" Will asked Pru.

"Lousy boxer," she said as she tilted her glass to her mouth. "He never did get on the bill as often as Finn, on account of he just didn't draw enough of a crowd. Finn's the one they all come out to see. He boxes two nights a week, Tuesdays and Saturdays. They set up the ring on the dance floor. It's just a four-dollar purse, but there's hundreds wagered in bets, thousands sometimes, if enough nobs show up."

"And they were both bouncers, too?" he asked.

"They were Mother's only bouncers," Pru said, her eyes bleary, her voice growing slurred. "Finn only bounces on his nights off from boxing, so on Tuesdays and Saturdays, it was Johnny's job. Finn bounces for the rent on the chicken house and boxes for his spendin' money. Johnny jus' bounced for a little bit of extra cash whenever he wasn't runnin' other stuff on the side for Mother."

"Such as…?" Will asked.

"Well, I know he looked after the wagering."

"On cards, you mean?" Nell asked. "The back room?"

"And the fights, which is more complicated, 'cause they're fixed, half of 'em." She winced. "Which I'm not s'posed to talk about, so please don't let Mother know I said anything."

"You have my word," Will said.

"There's also the hop joint downstairs," Pru said. "Johnny bought the gong and made sure the dope fiends had what they needed, the pipes and all the rest of it, and that the cops were paid to look the other way. And he did other stuff that didn't have anything to do with this place. Mother's got business all over this part of town."

"What kind of business?" Will asked.

"I couldn't say." Holding a finger to her lips, her head slightly wobbly, she said, "It's real hush-hush. I know she's got a stable of plug-uglies that do her bidding, but nobody really knows what they do. Johnny was her go-between with them. He'd do whatever Mother needed doin', is the gist of it. I heard he made a good penny at it."

"Then, of course, there was whatever Mary took in," Nell said. "You said he kept it all for himself?"

"Oh, yeah, sure, whatever her johns paid...and maybe the occasional fella that liked to watch, huh?" Pru said with a drunken chuckle.

"If Johnny was earning so much money," Nell asked, "why was he living downstairs in that...hole?"

Gesturing for Nell and Will to lean toward her, Pru said in a thick-tongued, gin-fumed whisper, "Finn tol' me Johnny was savin' his dough to open his own place right down the street, a concert saloon like this, but bigger and fancier. Said he was gonna give Mother a run for her money, steal away her customers and put the ol' bloater out of business. Can you 'magine?" she snickered.

"I don't guess that would have made Mother very happy," Nell said.

"How was she s'posed to find out," Pru asked in a tone that suggested Nell might be a little slow, "if Finn or Johnny didn't tell her? They're the only ones that know. Knew. You know what I mean."

"You know," Nell pointed out, wondering why she had to.

"Yeah, well, Finn was soused when he tol' us, or he never woulda said nothin', 'cause—"

"Us?" Nell said.

"Me and Ivy and Fanny. Finn had us over to the chicken house one night after hours for a lil' party."

"A party?" Nell said. "Three women and one…?" She got it as soon as the words were out of her mouth.

Now it was Will looking at her as if she were slow. With a smile that made her want to punch him, he said, "I'll explain the mathematics later."

"Finn was drunker than I ever seen him that night," Pru said. "Thas' why he tol' us, but he said it was s'posed to be a big secret. He made us promise to keep our mouths shut, said if we din't, he'd shut 'em for us permanent." She grinned and shook her head, as if to say, *Men.*

"But you're telling *us*," Will said.

Who knew how many people those three whores had already spilled the beans to, Nell wondered, and how many people those people had told. Divulged secrets tended to spread like a spider web.

Pru stared at Will for a long, hard moment, as if trying to get a bead on his face. Her look of dismay at having revealed such a dangerous secret evaporated fairly swiftly. With a dismissive wave of her hand, she said, "Finn won't mind. Johnny's dead. No reason to keep the secret anymore." She raised her glass, found it empty, and held it toward Will, waving it back and forth with an imploring pout.

Will held up two fingers to a passing waiter girl. His ersatz drinks, meanwhile, remained untouched.

"You're a prince, Tommy," Pru said. "Say, listen. The two of you ain't…you know…together, are you?"

"Um, no," Nell said.

Leaning toward Will, Pru said, in a throaty voice, "Then how's about you let me take you downstairs and thank you for all them lovely drinks?"

With an apologetic smile, Will lifted her hand, kissed her knuckles, and shook his head. He said, "I'm sorry, that won't be possible."

"You a gal-boy?" Pru asked.

"Yes, Pru, I am a gal-boy," he said with quiet gravity. "Were I not, how could I possibly resist the allure of one such as yourself?"

"Gimme a chance," she inveigled. "One night with me, and you'll look at women in a whole new light."

"I'm all too sure that's true."

"IT DOESN'T LOOK GOOD FOR Cook," Will said as they left Nabby's, arm in arm. It was around one in the morning, and there was, thank the fates, a cool breeze blowing off the harbor. North Street was, if not deserted, at least less populated than it had been earlier, and therefore a good deal less noisy and strident.

"It could be worse," Nell said.

"He was seen standing over a gunshot victim with his own revolver in his hand."

Nell said, "You, of all people, should know that being caught 'red-handed' doesn't automatically translate into guilt."

"But it does translate into the perception of guilt—as does his relationship with Mary Molloy. If Cook ever stands trial for this shooting, chances are he'll be found guilty."

"What about Shute?" she asked.

"What about him?"

"He lied to us, at least by omission. Not only did he return to Nabby's for a second visit, he was bodily thrown out by none other than the man who turned up dead the next night—a man whom he threatened in front of God knows how many witnesses."

"Perhaps," Will said, "he didn't tell us about the incident because he was simply embarrassed. It's humiliating enough to experience something like that. Perhaps he just wanted to put it behind him."

"Why do you suppose Johnny threw him out?" she asked. "He seems like such a civilized sort—refined, personable..."

"So do I, most of the time," Will said, slanting a smile in her direction. "So you see, my dear Cornelia, appearances *can* be deceiving."

"Do you think we're being deceived by Denny?" she asked.

"You mean, do I think he's a little pervert who's going to grow up to rape and pillage and plunder? No, I do not."

Will raised his hand and whistled, which was when Nell noticed a pair of carriage lamps down the street. The hack pulled up to the curb.

"Evenin' ma'am," said the driver with a little tip of his hat. "Sir. Where can I take you folks tonight?"

"One forty-eight Tremont," Will said as he handed Nell up into the rather shabby black carriage.

"Denny Delaney is a good kid with a normal curiosity about the fairer sex," Will said as he settled in beside Nell on the cracked leather seat. "Did he employ poor judgment in watching Mary unawares? Unarguably. But boys at that age are hardly known for their astute decisions, especially about matters having to do with women. I daresay, I committed far more egregious offenses at his age. If you knew the half of it, you'd have nothing to do with me, even now."

"I doubt that." She turned to smile at him. Will returned the smile as the light from a passing streetlamp fluttered across his face, dancing over the finely sculpted bones, the shadowed eyes. He had the kind of face that would age not just gracefully, but magnificently. Nell couldn't help wondering, in light of his unsettled existence and their strange, unresolved relationship, whether she would still know him when his temples were silvered, his eyes bracketed by creases.

The thought that she might not made her feel desperately empty inside.

"One thing I do know," Will said. "No adolescent boy deserves to be savaged by a bully like Finn Cassidy for an offense of that nature. And it's clear they sought no medical care at all for him afterward. The broken nose, well, that's not so bad. Imparts a certain hint of ruggedness that may end up serving him well with the ladies, given that he's so bookish. But that hand of his will never be fully functional. He'll have to live with that for the rest of his life."

"Well, where are we?" Nell asked. "What do we need to do next?"

"I'd say a little chat with Brian O'Donagh might be in order. We should pay a visit tomorrow to that pub where he keeps his office. The Blue...?"

"Fiddle," Nell said. "The Blue Fiddle. Richmond Street near Salem."

"Other than that, what we need to do is what we've needed to do all along, prove that Colin Cook didn't kill Johnny Cassidy. It won't be easy, what with three witnesses to swear that he did. The fact that two of them were drunk on opium at the time *should* cast their testimony into doubt, but if they're upper-crust types, and it seems as if they may be, they'll be believed regardless of their condition at the time. I wish to God we had their names so that we could find out what they told Skinner, and how badly it may hurt Cook."

"I have their names," Nell said with a smug little smile.

Will turned and stared at her, a gratifying look of incredulity in his eyes. "And you have them because..."

"After you went out front to pay Riley the rent...and sweet-talk the enchanting Pru...Mother Nabby needed the necessary, so I took her there. By the way, if you ever notice me gaining an extra few hundred pounds, do snatch the fork out of my hand with all due haste."

"I think the warning sign will be when you stop bothering with the fork."

"While I was walking her to the water closet," Nell said, "I pinched that little ledger she keeps in her pocket, the one where she keeps track of the nobs who pay on credit."

"Once a finger-smith, always a finger-smith," Will said laughingly. Drawing her toward him, he kissed her forehead. "I love you, Nell."

Everything stopped for about a second—all sound and sensation, even Nell's heartbeat. Scrambling for recovery, she said, "Um, while she was in the W.C., I looked through the book for entries dated July fifth, the night of the murder. One page had the names of two men, and a list of the things they owed her for—the opium and use of the all the paraphernalia, the smoking pistols, lamps, spindles, even the pillows."

"She charges for the pillows?"

"She charges for the pillows."

"Avaricious witch."

"It came to fourteen dollars apiece," Nell said.

"Pure thievery."

"The men we need to talk to are Lawrence Pinch and Ezra Chapman."

Frowning, Will said, "Why do I know those names?"

"They're friends of your brother's," Nell said.

"Harry," Will said glumly. He ducked his head and rubbed the bridge of his nose, breathing something Nell knew he didn't mean her to hear. "Harry's friends. Yes. Well. Harry's friends have always been much like Harry. Unfortunately."

"We should speak to Pinch and Chapman," Nell said. "Any idea how we might go about locating them?"

"Harry's chums have traditionally taken their lunch at the Somerset Club."

"Which is only open to members."

"I'm a Hewitt," Will drawled. "There's no door in Boston that is closed to us. I'll go to the Somerset tomorrow during the luncheon hour and pray that Pinch and Chapman aren't still abed, sleeping off their daily morning heads."

"I realize the Somerset is gentlemen only," Nell said. "I don't suppose they'd ever make an exception for—"

"Queen Victoria herself couldn't set foot in that place," he said. "Sorry, Nell. I'll do the best I can all on my own—although I shall miss your diverting company more than I can say."

CHAPTER TWELVE

"WILL IT EVEN BE OPEN this early?" asked Nell the next morning as Will knocked on the front door of the pub on Richmond Street in which Brian O'Donagh was said to hold court. With a glance at her pendant watch, she said, "It's barely ten o'clock."

It was the kind of place one might pass by without noticing, so small and undistinguished was its exterior, just a solid oak door with two heavily curtained windows to either side. The only clue that it was the place they sought was a very small sign in the shape of a fiddle, painted blue with gold trim, hanging to the side of the door.

"This is the North End, and taverns tend to be open at all hours here," Will said. "But if it's not, we'll just find a coffee shop and come back…" He tilted his head, listening. "Someone's coming."

There came the soft metallic click of a key turning in a lock, and then the door swung open about a foot, courtesy of a young red-headed man in shirtsleeves and a bib apron, holding a bottle brush. "Sorry, we ain't open yet," he said in a fresh-off-the-boat brogue. "You might come back at noon."

"We're here to see Mr. O'Donagh." Will handed him his card. "Miss Cornelia Sweeney and Dr. William Hewitt."

The young man, a bartender from the looks of him, surveyed them swiftly, taking in Will's black frock coat and top hat, Nell's dove-gray walking dress of fine silk twill—their normal attire, which Nell was relieved to return to. "Does Mr. O'Donagh expect you, then?"

"No," Will said, "but it's a matter of some importance."

"Sorry," said the bartender as he stepped back to shut the door. "He's busy."

Pressing a hand to the door to keep it from closing, Nell said, "Tell him it has to do with an old friend of his, Colin Cook. Please. I think he'll want to speak to us if he knows that."

The bartender hesitated a moment, then shut and relocked the door. From inside came the sound of his retreating footsteps, then silence. Nell and Will waited. An ice cart rumbled past, and another cart bearing kegs bound for one of the many local saloons. From the next street over came the competing cries of a newsboy and a woman hawking fresh fish.

Just when Will was fixing to pound on the door again, it opened. "This way," said the bartender as he ushered them inside. They followed him toward the rear of the pub, which was long and narrow, a clubby little haven lit by a row of pendant lamps over the bar. Nell breathed in the aromas of tobacco, bacon, and linseed oil.

The rear of the bar opened into a hallway, at the end of which, near a closed door, sat a strapping blond fellow reading a newspaper, a cup of coffee on a little table next to him. *A Viking in the big city*, Nell thought. He stood as they approached, his head nearly touching the ceiling, and appraised Nell and Will with the frankness of a cop—or a bodyguard. On his coat collar was a small gold and enamel badge featuring a shamrock overlaid with crossed swords and a little banner reading F.O.S.E. *Fraternal Order of the Sons of Erie.* Beneath his wool coat, Nell saw a bulge that could only have been a holstered pistol.

"This is them, Cormac," the bartender said, and left.

"Off with your coat, then," Cormac told Will. His accent was even denser than the bartender's.

The command stunned Nell, but Will took it in stride, almost as if he'd expected it. He set his hat on the table, after displaying its interior to show it was empty, shucked his coat, and handed it over for inspection. Without being asked, he turned to show that there were no weapons hidden behind him, then propped each foot on the chair to raise his trouser legs. Cormac patted him down, returned the coat, and turned to Nell.

"He'll want to see your reticule," Will told her, "and the contents of your pockets, if you have any." To the guard, he said, in a tone that brooked no argument, "And that's all you get to see."

Cormac searched Will's eyes for about a second, sizing him up the way a man does when he's trying to determine how much fight there might be in a potential adversary. Will met his gaze unflinchingly, with that predatory thrust to his jaw, his arms—much longer than Cormac's despite the guard's height and bulk—held in soldier-like readiness at his sides.

The guard nodded once and reached for Nell's little needle-point reticule, in which he poked around for a bit before handing it back. Nell had one hidden pocket in her voluminous skirt; she turned it inside out to show that it was empty.

"This door stays open," Cormac said as he gave it a soft rap. "Your callers, sir."

"Show them in, then," came a deep-chested command that bore a subtle Irish lilt.

The guard ushered them into a darkly masculine enclave furnished in leather and mahogany that reminded Nell of August Hewitt's private upstairs library, right down to the globe and the books. A polished banker's desk stood near the back wall before a damask-draped window, but its chair was empty. The man they came to see, handsomely attired but for a napkin tucked under his chin, was seated instead at a marble-topped table laid out with the remains of a morning repast of eggs, bacon, scones, strawberries, jam, and tea. He had a massive head, not unlike Detective Cook's, with neatly pomaded salt and pepper hair.

O'Donagh stood as his gaze lit on Nell, pulling away the napkin and ducking his head with a genial smile she wouldn't have expected, given what they'd had to go through to gain entrance to his private sanctum. She was immediately struck by the sheer, squared-off bulk of the man—not that he was heavyset, although he must have carried half again as much weight as Will. He was broad and thick-boned, with colossal shoulders housed in an exquisitely tailored coat, the lapel of which sported a little green and gold F.O.S.E. badge like that of his bodyguard.

"Miss Sweeney, is it?" O'Donagh said, wiping his hands on the napkin as he gestured for Nell and Will to join him at the table. "Any relation to Terence Sweeney from Oliver Street?"

"I shouldn't think so," Nell said as she lowered herself into the chair Will pulled out for her. "I'm from Cape Cod originally."

"But you weren't born there," he said as he retook his seat, smoothing down his coat.

She shook her head. "I was born in Falcarragh in County Donegal. But I only lived there for a year before—"

"Aha!" He slapped the table, rattling the dishes and silverware. "I knew it. I can always tell a blossom that sprouted in the old country. There's that intoxicating sparkle in the eyes, that blush of dawn upon the cheeks. Where on Cape Cod?"

"Oh. Um, Falmouth, mostly."

"Falmouth. Falmouth…There's a fella called…" He squinted across the room, drumming his giant fingers on the table. "Duncan. Duncan Sweeney. An associate of mine met him up at Charlestown State Prison a while back. He hails from Falmouth. You wouldn't be kin to him, by any chance?"

Nell stared at O'Donagh, astounded that he'd so swiftly made the connection to her estranged husband—her very secret estranged husband—and at a loss as to how to respond.

Will came to her rescue. "Miss Sweeney was quite young when she left Falmouth."

O'Donagh turned to Will, regarding him with a cool, assessing smile. "Doctor..." He slid a pair of spectacles onto his nose, lifted Will's card from the table, and slid the spectacles off. "Hewitt. Of *the* Hewitts, I take it."

"That is correct."

The big man sat back to appraise them, the smile frozen in place, speculating, no doubt, on the relationship between the Irish-born Miss Sweeney and the scion of one of Boston's most venerable old families.

"I serve as governess to the Hewitts," Nell said. "Dr. Hewitt and I are looking into a situation involving a man whom we're told is an old acquaintance of yours—Detective Colin Cook of the State Constabulary."

"Cormac!" O'Donagh called.

The door swung open. "Yes, sir."

"Have Paddy bring a pot of tea and a plate of scones for our guests."

"Right away, sir."

"Do you know Detective Cook?" O'Donagh asked.

"He's a friend of mine," Nell said. "Three nights ago, there was a murder at—"

"Yes," O'Donagh said with a wave of his hand. "Johnny Cassidy. And now Colin has disappeared with Cassidy's woman. Mary..."

"Molloy," Nell said.

"Molloy." O'Donagh nodded. "Not much happens in this neck of the woods that I don't hear about, Miss Sweeney. And, of course, I've had a good many personal dealings with Johnny Cassidy, given that he acted as liaison between Mother Nabby and those with whom she had business arrangements, so his killing is of particular interest to me."

As casually as she could, Nell said, "May I ask the nature of those business arrangements, Mr. O'Donagh?"

The big man gave her a forbearing smile. "A pretty lass may ask all sorts of things that others wouldn't dare to, Miss Sweeney, but I'm afraid you shan't find me very forthcoming on the subject. The activities of the Brotherhood are varied and complicated—and more importantly, prone to misinterpretation by those who think it a simple matter to see to the interests of the Irish in a hostile Brahmin enclave like Boston. Suffice it to say Mother and I share some ventures of mutual interest. Johnny facilitated those for her. He was her 'legs,' so to speak." Turning to Will, he asked, "You ever seen his brother box?"

"Never had the opportunity, no. I understand he's very good."

"I wouldn't bet against him, that's for sure."

Paddy, the red-headed bartender, delivered a tea tray and a plate of scones and left.

"I'm not responsible," said O'Donagh as he poured tea for Nell and Will, and a refill for himself.

"I'm sorry?" Nell said.

"For Johnny's death. I didn't do it, and I didn't order it done." He stirred a dollop of honey into his tea and reached for a wedge of lemon. "Just wanted to get that out of the way."

"Of course. So—"

"'Looking into it,'" O'Donagh said as he squeezed the lemon into his cup. "What does that mean, precisely? You tryin' to prove Colin didn't do it?"

"Yes," said Will.

"Who do you think did?"

"That's what we're trying to figure out," Nell said, "so that Detective Cook doesn't end up hanging for a murder he didn't commit."

Will said, "Your friendship with Cook goes back to the old country, yes?"

O'Donagh nodded. "We were both Young Irelanders, fought side by side till they started rounding us up for deportation, then we took ship for Boston."

Will said, "We know that Cook mined coal in Pennsylvania for a few years while you established the Sons of Erie here, and that when Cook came back to Boston, he worked for you."

"He was my righthand man, saw to various aspects of the Brotherhood's dealings."

"Such as?" Nell asked. Will glanced at her, looking amused, but also perhaps a little impressed by her persistence.

O'Donagh's smile was a bit tighter this time, a bit less indulgent. "Once again, Miss Sweeney, the Brotherhood's interests are many and complex."

She nodded and sat back, waiting. Will, bless him, knew better than to puncture the increasingly weighty silence.

O'Donagh smiled knowingly. "You learned this tactic from Colin, didn't you? He used to say, 'Ask a question, then keep your mouth shut and wait for the other fellow to give in and start talking. Most folks can't bear to sit and look at each other with no words to fill the air.' Well, I'm not most folks, Miss Sweeney, so I'm afraid you'll have a long wait ahead of you if you choose to employ that strategy."

She said, "Let me ask a simpler question, then, on the understanding that your answer will go no further than this room. The things Detective Cook did for you, were they by and large legal, or…?"

"If you know Colin, I think you know the answer to that question. Yes, Miss Sweeney, they were by and large legal—getting urchins off the streets, finding wharf jobs for the men and maidservice jobs for the women, feeding starving widows. The closest he ever came to the edge of the law was bracing the occasional landlord or boss."

"Do you mind telling us why he left the Brotherhood to join the Police Department?" she asked. *I know he was disgusted with the road they were taking,* Shute had said, *the tactics, the payoffs.*

"If you ask me, it all came down to Chloe."

"His wife?" Will said.

"She wasn't his wife then," O'Donagh said. "She was Daniel Duffy's wife."

Nell and Will glanced at each other. "Daniel Duffy?" Nell said.

"He was in the Brotherhood, one of the original members who formed my inner circle—my 'cabinet,' you might say. Danny was smart as a whip, and the most likeable fellow you ever met— when he was sober. But he had a real love affair with the bottle, and it changed him, made him surly."

"A mean drunk?" Will said.

"The meanest." O'Donagh shook his head, looking genuinely somber. "Anyway, the long and the short of it is that Colin went to Danny's place on Brotherhood business one evening and caught him beating up on Chloe. He knew it wasn't the first time—we'd all seen the marks on her—but Danny was in a particularly vicious mood that night. I saw her afterward, and, well…it's a wonder she lived through it, is all I can say. She might not have if Colin hadn't put a bullet in Danny."

"He killed him?" Will asked.

"Shot him, didn't kill him. He hit him in the chest, but missed the heart. Said it was the only way to stop him. Soon as Danny could travel, we put him on a steamer headed for the west coast. Chloe petitioned for a divorce on the grounds of desertion. It was a legal nightmare, took years and cost her everything she had, but—"

"Years?" Nell said. "It takes *years* to…?"

Will turned to look at her.

"Well, sure," said O'Donagh. "Divorces are hard to come by in this state. This is a subject I know something about. Several times over the years, I've been called upon to…exercise my connections with certain judges on behalf of local Irishwomen whose husbands abused them and their children—or, in one case, left the wife for another woman."

"These were Irish *Catholic* wives?" Nell asked.

"They knew they would never be able to remarry in the Church," O'Donagh said, "and they knew they'd have to live with the stigma afterwards, but at least they'd have the legal right to keep these bastards…" He glanced contritely at Nell. "Sorry."

"Not at all."

"They'd have the right to keep their former husbands out of their homes. But it's a long, torturous process, getting a Massachusetts court to grant a divorce decree—unless you're a Lowell or an Abbot, I suppose, and have plenty of cash and influence to throw around. Otherwise, it's hard enough even if both parties are agreeable, but if one of them fights it, or isn't around to fight it, 'specially the husband, it's nigh unto impossible. Few of those women I tried to help were able to get a divorce decree."

"I see," Nell said quietly.

"But luck was on Chloe's side—that, and she's one smart, determined lady. Her divorce finally came through, and after Colin returned from the war, she married him. I understand she made him stop drinking first, but you can hardly blame her for that."

"Hardly," Nell agreed, recalling Duncan's drunken rages, and the scars she'd wear for days afterward.

O'Donagh said, "It was after we shipped Danny away that Colin more or less fell out with the Brotherhood. He'd shot one of our own, and some of the boyos weren't all that sure it'd been called for. Not that he hadn't needed to be stopped, but with a bullet? There were whispers that Colin had been sweet on Mary before that, and just itching for an excuse to get Danny out of the way, but I never did believe that. It wasn't Colin's way. He's always been one for doing the right thing and choosing the right path— the godly path. Almost became a priest once, did you know that?"

"Mrs. Cook told us," Nell said.

"Was that the only reason for Cook's rift with the Brotherhood?" Will asked. "His shooting Daniel Duffy?"

"Well, Colin and I never did see eye to eye on the best way to do get things done," O'Donagh said. "I'm a pragmatic man. I do whatever it takes. Colin...well, he's a man of honor. He does the right thing, and the right thing only. Sooner or later, the two of us were bound to part ways, but I'm happy to say we didn't part enemies."

"But did you part friends?" she asked.

O'Donagh laced his fingers over his chest and sighed. "No, Miss Sweeney, I can't rightly call us friends anymore. Truth is, when we pass each other on the street, we nod and walk on by. I know what he thinks of me and the Brotherhood nowadays, and there's no forgetting who he works for now, and where his loyalties lie. I can't imagine we'll ever be on the same side again, fighting for the same cause. But back when we did, in the old country..." O'Donagh smiled wistfully, looking beyond them to a different time, a different land. "There was no man on God's green earth I would rather have had by my side than Colin Cook."

"WAIT HERE," WILL TOLD THE driver as he handed Nell out of a hack a discreet block and a half away from his parents' house around noon. "I'll be back in ten minutes, and then I'll be going to the Somerset Club."

"Do you really think this is necessary?" Nell asked as Will took her arm to walk her to the house. "It's midday, the sun is shining. I very much doubt that I'll be accosted by Skinner or his evil minions between here and Colonnade Row."

"I doubt it, too," he said, "but it is not, unfortunately, out of the question. There's also the issue of the house itself. What if someone broke in this morning while we were out, and is lurking in there, waiting to pounce?"

"And what do you think the chances are of that?" she challenged.

"What do you think the chances are of my concentrating on anything other than your welfare if I don't look through the house first and make sure there's no danger to you?"

Nell followed Will through the house as he made a swift but thorough search of every room, closet, pantry, W.C., stairwell, alcove, nook, and cranny. He tarried for a minute in his room, or rather, Gracie's room, in order to fetch some money with which to bribe his way into the Somerset Club in the unlikely event that his pedigree alone didn't do the trick.

Nell leaned on the door jamb, watching Will's reflection in a monumental, gilt-framed mirror as he unbuckled the old alligator satchel that held his gambling cash. He was almost cruelly handsome, with that height, those intense eyes, that lean, masculine grace.

Very early this morning, after lying awake in bed for some time listening to Will's somnolent breathing, Nell had risen and padded silently to the doorway separating the two rooms. The sanguine glow of dawn sifting through the curtains had imparted an otherworldly radiance to the sheet-draped furnishings, making them look like a range of snow-covered mountains. On the carpeted floor next to the bed lay the pair of white linen drawers he'd shucked off upon retiring for the night.

The frothy lace curtains surrounding Gracie's canopy bed had been tied back, revealing Will lying facedown with the sheet tangled around one long leg. The exposed leg, the right one, was the one with the deep, ragged scar puckering the quadriceps—from a bullet he'd removed himself shortly before his escape from Andersonville.

His face was turned toward Nell. Tendrils of hair hung over his eyes, and his mouth was half open, imparting an almost child-like aura, in striking contrast to his sinewy, ravaged body. She'd had to fight the urge to go over and brush the hair off his fore-head. He would have awakened, had she done that, lying naked in bed with her standing over him in her night shift. Touching him. Unthinkable.

Unthinkable.

"Nell? Don't you think so?"

"Um…I'm sorry. I've been…"

"Don't you think, if and when this case goes to trial, that the prosecution will have a field day with Cook's past? Having served as lieutenant to the likes of Brian O'Donagh was bad enough, but he actually shot a man for mistreating a woman, which may be exactly what happened Monday night."

Nell looked at him sharply.

"According to the D.A.," he hastily amended, meeting her gaze in the mirror with a pacifying smile.

"I knew Chloe wasn't telling us everything yesterday," Nell said. "She gave us to believe she hadn't really known Cook when he first came to Boston from Pennsylvania, said they'd met through 'mutual acquaintances.'"

"Not so much lies as equivocation," Will said. "She didn't want us to know that her husband shot Daniel Duffy for fear that we'd reach the conclusion any jury is likely to reach—that if Colin Cook is capable of shooting one woman-beater, he's capable of shooting another."

"Do you think he did it, Will?" she asked.

Turning to face her, he said, "I respect you far too much to lie and tell you I think it's impossible."

A helpless little whimper rose in her throat. "I hate this."

"I know," he said softly as he came to stand next to her, closing a hand over her arm. "Colin Cook is a lucky man, to have a friend like you. As am I."

NELL WATCHED FROM HER BEDROOM window as Will walked the block and a half to his waiting hackney and climbed into it.

She kept her gaze on the carriage until it was out of sight, and then, having reached a decision, she went downstairs and hailed a hack. "Charlestown State Prison," she told the driver.

CHAPTER THIRTEEN

❧

"**N**o," Duncan said.

"Duncan—"

"No!" He slammed both hands down on the scarred wooden table in the middle of the prison's little visitors' room, sending tremors not just through the table, but through Nell, sitting at the opposite end. Duncan's aquamarine eyes, the most striking feature of his devilishly handsome face, caught fire in a stripe of sunlight from the nearby window. "You're my wife."

"Duncan, we haven't lived as man and wife for ten—"

"That don't matter! How could that matter? We were married in the Church. The Church made us man and wife, and it can't ever be undone. Never!"

Nell had half-hoped, during the two years since she'd last seen Duncan, that his attachment to her would have lessened a bit. Clearly, that had been wishful thinking.

Struggling to keep her voice even, she said, "It can't be undone in the eyes of the Church, perhaps, but it can in a court of law. It won't be easy. The Hewitts mustn't find out. As you know, I've kept my marriage a secret from then, so I'll have to keep my divorce a secret, as well. It'll be all the more difficult if you contest it. It could take a great deal of time to secure a divorce decree, years perhaps, and it might cost every cent I've saved working for the Hewitts. But it's something I have to do."

"Why?" he demanded. "You fixin' on gettin' hitched again?"

"I have no such plans."

"It's *him*, ain't it? The son. The doctor."

"I told you," she said, cursing the uncanny insight, at least when it came to her, that had helped him to wield such absolute control over her in the beginning. "I have no such—"

"You bangin' him?"

"No." She shook her head in weary frustration. "Duncan, please. Just look at this from my point of view. Even if my marriage to you still felt…like a marriage, even if I still considered myself your wife, would you honestly expect me to wait twenty more years for you? That's how long you've got left on your sentence, with no possibility of parole."

"I coulda gotten paroled," he reminded her. "It was all set up. If I hadn't busted outa here two years ago, I'd be a free man already. I did it for you, to keep you from getting killed, and now you just want to toss me out with the trash?"

Nell closed her eyes, drawing a deep, steadying breath as her throat began to tighten. "Duncan, you know I'll always be grateful for that sacrifice, deeply, sincerely grateful. I'll never forget it."

She opened her eyes to find that sea-blue gaze searching hers, as if to capture some remnant of the affection they'd once shared for each other. Wresting her gaze from his, she stared through the barred window at the sun-washed courtyard and the two barnlike stone shops in which the prisoners made themselves useful to society. A pair of uniformed guards stood some distance away under a shade tree, smoking cigarettes. One of them was the guard who'd told her he'd be standing watch out in the hallway in case she needed anything.

No, she would never forget Duncan's selflessness in giving up his freedom to protect her; how could she?

But neither, unfortunately, could she ever forget the rages, the beatings, and that last, ferocious attack and ensuing miscarriage, which she'd barely survived. If not for Dr. Cyril Greaves, she wouldn't be sitting here now, trying to wheedle cooperation out of Duncan.

Dr. Greaves hadn't merely saved her life after infection had ravaged her womb. He'd taken her in, trained her in nursing, taught her history and French, how to appreciate opera and art and literature, how to write a letter and comport herself, and so much more. When she'd finally gone to his bed, she'd gone willingly, gratefully. He'd not only saved her, but remade her, so that when Viola Hewitt realized she needed a governess for her adopted infant, Nell was a natural choice.

Every evening, upon retiring, Nell whispered her thanks to God for having brought Gracie into her life. Without the little girl she'd come to think of as her own, she couldn't imagine how empty she would feel, looking ahead to decades of child-lessness. She'd always wanted babies, even when she was little more than a baby herself. "You were born to do that," Nell's mother would say as she watched her daughter cuddle and feed and diaper the homemade rag doll that eventually disintegrated, despite dozens of mendings, from a surfeit of constant nurtur-ing. But by then she had Tess, the baby sister whose care had fallen to her when cholera claimed their mother and most of their siblings. Little Tess, her darling, sweet, impish little Tess, had succumbed herself to diphtheria in the Barnstable County Poor House when she was just three years old, leaving Nell lost and bereft...until Duncan.

Nell's mum was right; she *had* been born to be a mother. It was the one thing she'd always yearned for, the one bone-deep, primal drive that she'd ever felt. It was, in a word, her destiny—a destiny Duncan Sweeney stole from her in his last vicious, snarl-ing, inexcusable assault.

It *had* been inexcusable, no matter what the priests said about pardon and absolution. "Forgive us our trespasses," Nell prayed every morning, "as we forgive those who trespass against us." And she meant it. With one single exception.

"If you'll never forget what I did for you," Duncan said, "givin' up my parole and all that, how can you want to divorce me?"

Still gazing out the window, she said softly, "There's a lot I can't forget, Duncan."

You gonna leave me, Nell? Huh? You want to leave? You can leave when I'm done with you. She forced herself to relive it—the punches and kicks, the sting of the knife, the horror as he ripped open her basque and threw up her skirts. *I'm gonna make it hurt,* he'd growled. And it had. It had hurt her horribly.

It had killed their baby.

"I'm sorry, Nell," he said in a voice raw with feeling. "I can't ever make it up to you, what I took from you, but I've changed. You know I have."

I've changed, Nell. I'm gonna stop drinkin'. I'll make it up to you. I'll be different from now on...

God, I'm sorry, Nell. Please give me another chance, please, I'm beggin' you, just one...

You don't deserve me, but I love you so much. I don't know what I'd do without you. Just one more chance...

It was the booze. I'm really stopping this time. I won't happen again. You'll see...

"Nell...darlin'. Say somethin'," he implored. "Please."

"I...I'm asking for your help so that I can move on with my life," she said. "If I can petition for the divorce in both our names, instead of you fighting it, there's a much better chance of it being granted, and it won't take nearly as much time or—"

"Don't do this, Nell. Don't do this to us." He stood with his arms braced on the table, leaning toward her, imploring her with those eyes she'd once thought of as most exquisite she'd ever seen, the eyes of a young god, now shimmering wetly. His forearms, revealed by the rolled-up sleeves of his striped prison shirt, were ropy and dusted with powdered granite; a vein pulsed on his forehead.

"Duncan," she said earnestly, "please don't make this more painful than it has to—"

"Jesus, Nell. *Christ.*" He scrubbed a hand over his eyes as the tears spilled out, leaving the upper part of his face smeared with granite dust. "You're all I got anymore," he said in a low, quavering voice, his arms shaking. "I ain't got nothin' else, *nothin'.* Nothin' but this place, this...purgatory. All I do all day is chop stone and think about you and how marryin' you was the only good and smart thing I ever done in my life, even if I did muck it up. That's it, that's all I got. Just you. Jesus, Nell, don't take that away from me, I'm beggin' you."

She squeezed her eyes shut—*I'm gonna make it hurt*—then opened them and stood, pushing her chair back. "You'll, um, you'll be sent some papers at some point. I would appreciate it very much if you would just sign them and—"

"No!" Duncan seized the table and hurled it aside, two legs cracking off as it hit the wall. "Goddamn it, no!"

Nell backed away from him so frantically that she tripped over her chair and landed in a heap of silk and crinoline, her left arm taking the brunt of the fall. She sucked in a breath to call the guard, not knowing whether he was even within earshot, but Duncan was on her in an instant, one hand gripping her wrists, the other clamped over her mouth as he straddled her. He leaned down so close that she could see her own eyes, wide with fear, reflected in the scalding blue of his.

"You gonna serve me with papers, Nell?" he demanded, teeth bared, his fingers digging into her jaw so hard she wondered if she'd be left bruised. "Are you? Huh?"

Nell squirmed and thrashed, trying vainly to throw him off, break his grip, scream for the guard...but to no avail. A decade of stonecutting had left Duncan even brawnier than he'd been before.

"If I get them papers, darlin'," he murmured, "you know the first thing I'm gonna do? Do you? I'm gonna write a letter to Mr. and Mrs. August Hewitt, one forty-eight Tremont Street, Boston, Massachusetts, tellin' 'em all about how me and *Miss* Nell Sweeney been married twelve years, and how you was once the very best pickpocket in all of Cape Cod, maybe all of Massachusetts, and how you been humpin' ol' Dr. Willie on the sly for God knows how long."

Nell bucked, loosening his grip on her mouth just enough for her to sink her teeth into his palm, good and deep.

He recoiled, swearing savagely. "You little—"

"Guard!" she screamed as she whipped a fist across Duncan's nose, spattering both of them with blood.

Duncan howled, hands cupping his nose, as the door slammed open. Both guards who'd been smoking under the tree leapt on him and heaved him off of her, kicking and flailing and spewing blood.

"I'll do it!" he screamed nasally as they wrestled him out of the room and down the hall. "Don't you think I won't, you ungrateful little bitch! You try and divorce me, I'll tell 'em everything! Every last goddamn thing! You'll be ruined! You hear me? Ruined!"

COMING HOME, NELL HAD THE driver leave her off on Bedford Street, cutting through an alley, a neighbor's stable yard, and the Hewitts' sunny rear garden to get to the back door. Listening to her footsteps echo off the marble floor of the central hall, she was struck, as always, by the sense of hollowness in the huge, empty house. With its windows thickly curtained and no lamps lit, it was as dark inside as if it were nighttime, even on a sunny afternoon like this.

As she passed the music room, there came a squeak of wood, as of someone rising up from that hundred-year-old duet stool next to the piano.

"Will?" Nell turned, seeing a shadow at the edge of her vision, darting behind her. She opened her mouth to scream.

A hand covered her mouth, pressing her head back against a meaty shoulder.

"Shh," he whispered into her ear.

CHAPTER FOURTEEN

"**D**ON'T SCREAM, MISS SWEENEY, PLEASE. It's me, Colin Cook."

Detective Cook? It was his voice; there was no mistaking it. Nell nodded, trembling with relief.

He took his hand off her mouth, supporting her for a moment by gripping her upper arms as she regained her bearings.

"What the devil...?" she began.

He came around to stand in front of her, a black-haired behemoth with an outsized head, his eyes huge in the gloom. His face and hands were dusky with soot, and his cap and clothing were that of a common laborer—a chimney sweep, Nell realized when she noticed the distinctive, long-handled brush leaning against the wall.

"I'm sorry to have startled you like that," he said in his time-worn brogue, "but I mustn't let anyone find out I'm here. You know I'm a wanted man. Mrs. Cook...She said you came to the house, you and Dr. Hewitt, and that you're tryin' to—"

"Yes," Nell said, rubbing her shaky arms. She winced when she touched her left elbow, which had taken the worst of it from her tumble onto the floor of the visiting room at the state prison. Her sleeve was torn open there, and stiff with blood. "Will and I are looking into things. We...we went to Nabby's Infero last night, and—"

"Later," he said, his grip on Nell's arms tightening. "You can tell me later. Mrs. Cook...she needs you. I think..." His eyes glimmered in the dark; his throat moved. "I think she's losing the baby."

"Oh, no," Nell said.

"I snuck back home this morning, just before dawn, 'cause I was worried about her. Turned out she'd already taken ill."

"In what way?" Nell asked.

"Cramping, a little bleeding."

"Just a little?"

"What's a little and what's a lot? I've no idea. I went and fetched Lily Booth, her friend, to stay and keep and keep an eye on her, and then I went lookin' for her doctor, this fella Mathers, but he's left town for the weekend. A sign on the door said to see Dr. Silk, over on Beacon Street, so I went to see him, but he was lunching at the Tremont Hotel, so I went there." Cook shook his head in exasperation. "I found him, finally, but he was eating, and you could tell he didn't want to be bothered. He said it didn't sound like there were any 'alarming symptoms,' and just to have her lie down, and 'all will pass off naturally.' Thing is, we been that route, the missus and I, and I ain't about to let her go through that hell again if there's anything to be done. She said you knew of a way, some Injun tonic or something..."

"A herb," Nell said. "Black haw. I have some. I use it for...I have occasional uses for it." Nothing else had proven as successful at easing her monthly cramps. Some black haw tea and a glass of wine were generally enough to keep her on her feet. "Give me a minute fetch it and leave a note for Dr. Hewitt. I'll be right back."

"I WANT TO THANK YOU for what you been doin', you and Dr. Hewitt," Cook told Nell as he drove her in his buggy to Fayette Street. They must have presented an odd image, a well-dressed young woman sitting next to a soot-covered chimney sweep, but at least he wasn't recognizable. "Can't say I was all that surprised, when Mrs. Cook told me. You always been one to stick your neck out, but I never thought you'd have to stick it out for me. I'm that grateful, Miss Sweeney. Just wanted you to know that."

"I appreciate that, Detective. I take it you realized you were a wanted man when you came home. You said you sneaked back."

"I heard 'em upstairs at Nabby's that night, screamin' for the cops, and I knew how it must have looked," he said. "Mrs. Cook tells me Skinner's on the warpath. She told me how he talked to her. However this turns out, I aim to get that little blowhard alone and put a fist in that big mouth of his. Let's see him try that kind of thing with no teeth in his head."

"Don't do that—" Nell began.

"With all respect, I don't reckon you could stop me."

"—without me there to watch."

Cook threw his head back and laughed, inadvertently jerking on the reins in a way that made the horses clatter to a stop on the cobblestone road. He got them moving again and said, "You remind me of Mrs. Cook when you say things like that. I told her once I thought you and her could be friends if you were ever to meet."

"I like her enormously," Nell said. "It's awful, what she's been through these past few days."

"It's my fault," Cook said as he negotiated a corner. "I never shoulda took that job with the state constables. The hours, the dangers…It's been hard on her all along, and now this." He shook his head gravely.

"I'm going to ask you something frankly," Nell said, "and I hope, as a friend, that you'll give me a frank—"

"Mary Molloy was never anything to me but a snitch," Cook said resolutely. "I can't tell you how it felt, hearin' what that bastard Skinner—'scuse the language."

"Feel free, when it comes to him."

"And she believed it, poor thing, or accepted it, anyways. But she knows the truth of it now, all of it."

"Which is…?"

"There's a whole network of crooks up in the North End, everything from street prowlers and common cutters right on up to them that do murder for hire. They buy opium off the ships and sell it to the hop joints. They fence stolen goods, run cons and extortions, lend money to gamblers and break their legs when they can't pay…It's like a family, almost, and every day it goes unchecked, it only gets more organized and powerful. Brian O'Donagh's one of the big potatoes. Mother Nabby's another one. They do some business on their own and some together. This Johnny Cassidy, the one that got shot, he saw to Mother's end of things."

"What did he do, exactly?" Nell asked.

"That's what I was payin' Mary to find out," Cook said, "on account of Major Jones is plannin' a big raid to clean up this mess once and for all, but we can't do it if we don't know what we're lookin' for. It was my job to gather information. I'd go see Mary when Johnny wasn't around, peel off a few greenbacks, and she'd tell me whatever she'd managed to squeeze outa him since my last visit."

"Pretty dangerous for her," Nell observed.

"Johnny woulda snuffed her out like a candle if he'd found out. He was a hard ticket if ever there was one, used to threaten to kill her in some pretty nasty ways if she ever tried to leave him—not so much 'cause he liked having her around, but 'cause she made money for him, lots of it. That's why he kept her penniless, so she'd have nowhere else to go."

Nell shivered despite the warmth of the afternoon. This scenario was all too reminiscent of Duncan's obsessive control over her during the two years of their marriage.

"That's why she narked for me," Cook said, "so as to save up enough dough to get away from Johnny and settle down someplace he'd never find her. I didn't know that till a couple of days ago, after I got her away from Nabby's. I didn't know how bad he was beating her, either, but I should have. I should have known all them bruises couldn't have been just from the badger game. I was closing my eyes to it, not thinking about it, 'cause she was giving me so much good information."

"The badger game?"

"It was the con they ran—or rather, Johnny ran it and made her play her part."

"A young girl in schoolgirl frocks and braids."

Cook nodded, a disgusted look on his face. "'Chickens,' they call 'em, or 'fresh greens.' There's some men go in for that—don't ask me why. She'd set there with her milk and her freckles, waitin' for a prosperous lookin' type to come on over and start chattin' her up. She'd get him drunk and let him take her downstairs to that basement room."

"And a minute or two later, Johnny would head down there," Nell said.

"After getting the key to the coal cellar from Mother Nabby, 'cause he'd made a spy hole to watch her play the mark."

"Mother was in on it, of course," Nell said.

Cook nodded. "He'd owe her a cut of the take from the con. Anyway, once Mary and the mark were on the bed with their clothes half off, Johnny'd burst into the room screamin' about how he was her father, and she'd disgraced him. He'd deal her a few blows, usually, to make it look good—bloody her nose, split her lip. The mark, would be shakin' in his boots, of course. Johnny was almost as scary as that brother of his. He'd threaten to beat the fella to a pulp or have him brought up on charges of seducing a girl under the age of consent—or both. In other words, he'd ruin the fella's life."

"Unless he paid up."

"And it would take a mountain of greenbacks to make the problem go away, whatever Johnny thought the mark could afford, and then some."

"What happened Tuesday night?" Nell asked. "Did it have something to do with the badger game?"

"I wish I knew. Tuesday night's fight night, and that's when I liked to go see Mary, on account of Johnny would usually be upstairs runnin' the bets. They were into the second fight when I got there. I sneaked down the back stairs, as usual, and found Mary packin' her things and Johnny on the floor with a bullet in his head. First thing I did was draw my weapon, 'cause I didn't know who shot him, and if he was still around. I even thought for a second Mary might have done it, but I looked around, and there was no gun. They got an errand boy at Nabby's, kid name of Denny Delaney, and he's standin' in the doorway with his eyes big as saucers—"

"Denny?" she said. "He was there? He told me he was upstairs when it happened." Or he'd led her to assume that.

"No, he was there, but Mary yelled at him to go upstairs and make like he was never down there, for his own good. She was always like a little mother hen to him, the only friend he had in that place. He said, 'But what about you?' and that's when she kinda turned and I saw how bad she'd been beat up. The whole right side of her face was all bloodied. She said she was all right, and he should worry about himself."

"So he left?"

"First he asked me if I was gonna look after her, get her away from there and get her fixed up. I said I would, and then he left. He's a good kid, that Denny. I hate to see him in a place like Nabby's, running and fetching for slamtrash like that."

"He should be in school," Nell said.

"I know. Problem is, he won't take anything from anybody. I offered to have him live with Mrs. Cook and me, told him I'd send him to Boston College High School—on account of it's a Catholic school, and he don't like the way the Catholic kids are treated in the public schools. He was tempted, I could tell, but he wouldn't hear of it, 'cause it'd be charity. I said he could do odd jobs around the house to earn his keep and the tuition, but he saw through that. He told me he knew could never work off what it'd cost to go to that school."

"It was very generous of you to make the offer, though."

Cook lifted those big shoulders. "It was the right thing. You want to sleep at night, you gotta at least try."

"What happened after Denny left the flat?" she asked.

"Well, I checked Johnny to make sure he was dead. No question about it. I asked Mary who done it, but she wouldn't tell me. Said, 'Don't ask me, please just don't ask me.' She said she had to get outa there, go someplace far away, 'cause if she stuck around there, chance were she wouldn't be alive that time tomorrow."

"So you left with her?"

"Yeah, but not soon enough. One of the bar girls saw us, and a couple of young hop heads. The girl went tearin' upstairs, and I heard her yellin' about Johnny Cassidy bein' murdered, and how she seen who done it. That's when I knew I had to take Mary and get us as far away as I could, 'cause they'd be comin' after me. The North End is Skinner's beat. I knew he'd leap at the chance to slip that noose around my thick Irish neck."

"So he has," Nell said. "Where is Mary now?"

"On a train headed west. She has a cousin in Chicago that Johnny never knew nothing about, nor anyone else. She wants to open her own flower shop—that's what she's been saving up for, so she can support herself and never have to be under the thumb of some bruiser like Johnny again. That's why she snitched for me."

"Did she actually manage to save enough to do that?" Nell asked.

Cook hesitated. "I, uh, helped her out with a little something extra."

She patted him on the back. "You're a good man, Detective."

"I felt bad for using her like I did, and ignoring the fix she was in."

Nell said, "I don't suppose she ever told you who killed Johnny."

"I never did get it outa her."

"Any theories?" she asked.

"None that add up all the way. Thing is, it coulda been just about anyone. Don't forget, Nabby's is overrun with bad pennies. There's a constant flow of 'em in and out of that place. And the basement flat has that outside entrance, so anybody coulda just snuck in, done the deed, and snuck right out again without bein' seen."

"Maybe it wasn't a bad penny," Nell said. "Maybe it was a bad shiner. The better element goes there, too."

"That they do."

"Such as your friend Ebenezer Shute."

Cook slanted her a look, then returned his gaze to the road. "Ben didn't have anything to do with Johnny Cassidy's murder, if that's what you're thinking. He came there the one time with me."

"And became captivated with Mary."

"Not at first," Cook said quickly. "Not when he thought she was some young kid. He noticed her over there in her corner and asked me what a girl that young was doing at a place like Nabby's. I told him she was about a decade older than she seemed, and it was only after that that he started lookin' at her…that way. He asked me if she was in the life."

"A hooker, you mean?"

Cook nodded as he drove. "I said not strictly speaking, but that if he made the mistake of havin' a go at her, he'd end up paying a far bigger price than if he just went for one of the other girls."

"You didn't tell him about the badger game?"

Shaking his head, Cook said, "I didn't tell my own boss about it. It was a major con, a felony, and Mary coulda ended up spending a lot of years behind bars if word started getting around. I just told Ben if he knew what was good for him, he'd keep his distance from Mary Molloy, no matter how tempted he was. But the more he drank, the more he wanted her. Couldn't hardly talk about anything else, so I finally drug him outa there for his own good."

"And took him to an oyster bar," Nell said.

Cook glanced at her, looking impressed. "You really woulda made one heck of a police detective, Miss Sweeney, if only you'd been born male. Yeah, I wanted to get some food into him, sober him up. I ordered four dozen of those nice little briny Cotuits from the Cape, but he just picked at 'em, and wouldn't even eat the bread. He tossed down about a gallon of ale, though, and by the time we parted company, he wasn't feelin' no pain."

"Did you know he was headed back to Nabby's?" Nell asked.

Cook grimaced. "Not at the time, no. I put him in a hack. I thought he was goin' home. I had to stick around the North End for a while, 'cause I had business at a gambling hell on North Street, couple of blocks up from Nabby's. I finished up there, and I'm walkin' down the street lookin' for a hack for myself, when who do I see but Ben limping toward me, looking madder than a jarful of wasps. He showed me his hands—they were scraped raw. His knee, too, right through his trousers."

"From being thrown out by Johnny Cassidy," Nell said.

"Yeah, he told me he'd gone back to Nabby's and gotten Mary to take him down to her room. They were on the bed, uh, you know, fiddlin' 'round, when Johnny throws the door open and—course, Ben didn't say 'Johnny.' He didn't know who it was, just said 'some wild-eyed bludger.' Johnny hauls him off Mary and throws him into the wall, gives Mary a couple of whacks. Ben said he tried to stop him from hitting her, but he was too boiled to be of any use. Johnny starts railin' about Ben takin' advantage of his thirteen-year-old daughter, and how he's gonna have to pay a thousand bucks to keep it quiet, else he can answer to the cops. He said he knew who Ben was, he'd been seen inspecting pawn-shops on North Street, and he'd be destroyed when it came out that he had a taste for underage girls."

"But he doesn't, right? I mean, he knew Mary wasn't really that young."

"Right, so he said go ahead and call the cops. He said he knew Mary wasn't any thirteen years old, and he wasn't paying one red cent. Johnny says fine, then, if he doesn't pay up within twenty-four hours, him and his pals will track Ben down and smash his good leg so bad that he'd lose that, too, plus his right arm, and they'd put out his other eye, for good measure. Ben told him he was bluffing. Johnny says, 'You call me, you'll see I ain't,' and he drags Ben upstairs and tosses him into the street."

"Whereupon Ben threatened to kill him, in front of witnesses."

Cook let out something that sounded like a sigh crossed with a groan. "Like I said, he was sizzled. It was an empty threat, the kind drunks make."

"Are you sure?"

"I am, as a matter of fact. After Ben told me all this, he asked me 'Do you think I'm in any real danger from this fella,' and I said 'Hell, yeah…' 'Scuse me."

"Not at all."

"I said, 'Yeah, you're in danger.' I told him I knew this fella, and he'd done worse than maiming people, he'd been known to do murder for fifty bucks, and not to even think about calling his bluff."

"A thousand dollars is a lot of money," Nell said. "I know Ben is well-set, but could he afford—"

"He's better than well-set," Cook said. "He's a millionaire several times over. It wasn't his wallet that'd end up hurtin', it was his pride."

"Did he agree to pay?"

"Not in so many words, but by the time we parted that night, I was pretty sure he'd bit the bullet and decided to do the smart thing."

"Does Ben Shute carry a gun?" Nell asked.

Cook gave her a look. "No, Miss Sweeney, he does not."

"But given his familiarity with pawnbrokers, he'd know where to get one. And as a former soldier, he'd know how to use it."

"Ben Shute did not kill Johnny Cassidy," Cook said as he turned onto Fayette Street.

"I wish I could share your..." Nell trailed off as Cook's house came into view at the other end of the block. The maidservant, Maureen, was standing out front, looking anxiously up and down the street, her arms wrapped around herself. She spied their buggy, waved her arms and pointed toward them, then backed away, crossing herself, as they approached.

"Detective..." Nell sat up straight, gripping the side of the buggy as she watched shapes move through the sheer curtains in the first floor windows of his house.

"That's our maid, Maureen. Something's wrong," Cooks said as he flicked the reins, urging the horses to speed up. "It's Chloe. Something's gone wrong with—"

"I don't think so." Nell said, clutching his sleeve as he pulled up in front of the house. "Don't stop. Keep going."

"What? But Chloe..."

The curtains parted in an upstairs window of Cook's house. An angular blond woman—Chloe's friend Lily Booth, Nell presumed—leaned out and screamed, "Colin! Go!"

The front door swung open and two blue-uniformed constables, one of them Skinner, came sprinting out with their guns drawn.

CHAPTER FIFTEEN

THREE OTHER CONSTABLES DARTED OUT of an alley across the street; and another popped out from behind a tree.

Cook snapped the reins, but two of the cops already had a grip on the horse's harnesses. They bucked and whinnied, but stayed put.

"Step down with your hands in the air," Skinner ordered Cook as he strode toward the buggy, pistol raised. "No going for your weapon, or I put a bullet in your head just like you did to ol' Johnny."

"Stay here," Cook implored Nell in a low, earnest voice as he grasped her arm. "Take care of Chloe. Save our baby, I'm begging you."

"Now, Cook!" Skinner yelled as he circled around to the driver's side, his pistol aimed, two-handed, at Detective Cook's head.

"I'll do my best," Nell promised, covering his hand with hers. "Just take care of yourself, Colin. This bastard's itching for an excuse to shoot you. Don't give him the satisfaction—for your wife's sake, if not for yours."

"I THINK I CAN SAY, with some assurance, that you're well out of the woods," Will told Chloe Cook as he tucked the bedcovers around her the next morning. "Your baby's heartbeat is strong, and you've had no contractions since…" He turned to Nell, standing with Lily Booth at the foot of Chloe's bed. "When would you say they stopped?"

"Early yesterday afternoon," Nell said.

"Right after her first cup of black haw tea," Lily added.

The first thing Nell had done after Cook's arrest yesterday, even before coming upstairs to check on Chloe—Lily was with her, after all—was to put a kettle on to boil. She prepared a particularly strong infusion of the potent herb, sweetened with honey to disguise the bitter taste, with which to dose Chloe at regular intervals.

By the time Will arrived in the late afternoon, Chloe's cramping and bleeding had ceased. Anxious though she was over the welfare of her husband, ratted out by Maureen for a handful of shiners, she at least had the comfort of knowing that her babe was still safe and sound in her womb.

"Nell…" Chloe, exhausted after her ordeal, but with the color returning to her cheeks, extended her hand.

Nell came to her side and took it.

"I owe you more than I could possibly repay," Chloe said.

Squeezing her hand, Nell said, "I'll leave a supply of black haw here. At the first little twinge—"

"Don't worry," said Lily, who'd resolved to move in and take care of Chloe until her baby was safely delivered. "I'll make a pot of it first thing every morning, just in case."

"The most important thing," Will told Chloe, "is to rest and keep your mind as tranquil as possible. Don't fret about your husband. Believe me, we'll be moving heaven and earth to free him."

"Go, then," Chloe said. "I'll be fine. I have Lily here. Go and do what you have to do to bring him home to me." Stroking a hand over her stomach, she said, "Me and the baby."

THE MORNING SUN FELT SEARINGLY bright as Nell and Will walked down Fayette toward Pleasant Street, where they hoped to find a hackney. She rubbed her eyes, raw from having stayed up all night, and wondered if she looked as bedraggled as she felt.

Will looked much as he always did, with the exception of one or two errant locks of hair and a creased frock coat from when he dozed off in a chair in the corner of Chloe's room for about an hour.

"Where to from here?" she asked around a yawn.

"Palazzo Hewitt, so you can take a much-needed nap," he said.

"What about you? Aren't you tired?"

"Not especially. I had that little cat-nap, remember, and I suspect I'm a good deal more accustomed than you to going without sleep—the cardsharp's lot, you know. I'll stop at the house to wash and change, and then I'll try to find out whether Cook's been arraigned yet, and if so, whether the judge granted bail."

"Do you think he will have?"

"I think it's extremely unlikely, given that Cook has already proven his propensity for flight, but anything's possible. I'll make sure he's got a good attorney, though."

"The best one you can find," Nell said. "He'll need it."

Will's conversation with Larry Pinch and Ezra Chapman at the Somerset yesterday had only served to tighten the noose around Detective Cook's neck. The two young men had, indeed, seen Cook standing over Jimmy Cassidy with his gun drawn, had taken him for the murderer, and were prepared to testify as such. They were, according to Will, entirely as arrogant and dissipated as their friend Harry Hewitt, but despite that and their opium use, he had no doubt that their social standing would add an aura of veracity to their testimony when the case went to trial.

"Given that Ben Shute was heard threatening Johnny Cassidy's life Monday night," Nell said, "it might not be a bad idea to pay another visit to Nabby's later this evening to find out if anyone can recall having seen him come back Tuesday. If he was as furious as Detective Cook said he was, perhaps he—"

"Nell." Grabbing her arms to halt her, Will turned her to face him, his gaze on the bodice of her gray silk dress, which she'd been wearing since yesterday. "What's this?" he asked, frowning at reddish-brown specks half-hidden amid the French piping that formed a *V* from shoulders to waist. They would have been nearly impossible to see in the dimly lit interior of the Cooks' house, but in the harsh light of day, there could be no mistaking what they were.

"This isn't *your* blood, is it?" Will asked.

"No. No, it's..." Nell hesitated, trying to imagine how Will would react to this. "It's Duncan's."

His jaw dropped. "Duncan *Sweeney?* Your husband?"

"I, um...I went to see him yesterday, at the prison, after you left for the Somerset—"

"You *what?*"

"I just...I needed to—"

"By *yourself?*" he asked incredulously, clutching her arms just a bit too tightly. "Here I've been trying so hard to keep you safe, and you...What were you thinking, Nell? Why in God's name would you have gone off without me—"

"To tell him I want a divorce."

Will stilled, staring at her as if he couldn't quite trust his ears. He eased his grip on her arms, stroking them lightly; he didn't even seem aware he was doing it. "Really? Wh-what about...the Catholic thing?"

"I've been doing a lot of thinking about it, Will—quite a lot, actually, and...you're right. God would never turn his back on me. The problem isn't that, not anymore. The problem is Duncan."

"He doesn't want to give you up." This was old territory.

"He says I'm all he has. But every time I start to feel a little sorry for him, I...well, I'm reminded of why I left him in the first place."

Frowning at the blood spatters on her dress, Will said, "What happened?"

"He became unhinged when I told him I'd be serving him with divorce papers. I had to punch him in the nose."

"Nell, Nell, Nell…" Cupping her face in his hands, Will said, "I'm proud of you for holding your own, very proud, but I don't ever want you putting yourself in that position again. The man is unbalanced. There's no reason you should ever have to deal with him again, certainly not alone. If you ever feel as if you have to go there, I'll come with you."

"I can't imagine that would put him in a more conciliatory frame of mine," Nell said dryly.

"I don't care about his frame of mind. I care about you. As for the divorce, if he fights it, fight him back. I'll find you the best lawyer in the commonwealth. We'll—"

"It's not that simple, Will."

"The money, you mean? I'll pay for it."

"Oh, Will, I couldn't let you—"

"For pity's sake, Nell," he said testily. "Aren't we beyond that?" He looked away for a moment, as if to compose himself. Stroking her cheek, he said, in a gentler voice, "The money doesn't mean anything to me. It's faro swag. Why shouldn't it come in good for something other than bankrolling more faro? I know it won't be easy to secure a divorce with Duncan opposing it. I know it'll take time and you'll have to do it in secret, but—"

"That's the problem," she said. "I won't be able to keep it a secret. He's not going to just oppose me, Will. He's going to tell your parents. He's going to write a letter to them, telling them about my marriage and my past, picking pockets and all that."

"Bloody hell." Will looked off down the street, rubbing his neck as he thought it through. He closed his eyes, whispering,

"Bastard." It was more swearing that he'd ever permitted himself in her presence.

"If they find out what I've been keeping from them," Nell said, "especially your father, I'll be ruined. Destroyed. I'll lose everything. My position in their household, my livelihood, my home, my reputation...Your father loathes me. He'll badmouth me far and wide. I'll be a pariah. But worst of all, I'll lose Gracie. I'll never be allowed to see her again. Your father might even try to send her away, as he did you when you were little. You know I can't risk that."

"There...there must be some way," Will said desperately, "something we can do to free you from this, this..."

"I've thought about it from every angle, Will, and if there *is* a way, it's beyond my ken. Twelve years ago, I took a vow to unite myself with Duncan till death do us part. It looks as if God is holding me to my word."

CHAPTER SIXTEEN

I T WAS SATURDAY NIGHT—FIGHT NIGHT, as Nell and Will were reminded by the bloodthirsty roar that greeted them as they crossed the threshold of Nabby's Inferno. Although the boxing match was taking place in the dance hall at the rear of the building, the screams of "Kill him!" and "Trounce the bastard!" resounded in Nell's skull as if she were standing in the middle of the ring.

Riley, the bartender, nodded as they walked over to him, a vague disappointment in his gaze as he surveyed Nell's attire. She wore the same gaudy tournure skirt of Mary Agnes's that she'd had on Thursday night, but with a lace-trimmed white blouse of her own. Even with the top few buttons undone, it was a considerably more modest, if still somewhat humble, costume.

After a couple of minutes of small talk, Will asked Riley if he happened to have noticed the one-legged fellow Johnny Cassidy threw out of the saloon Monday night. "I wasn't here," Will said in his provincial Boston accent, "but I heard about it. Thing is, he sounds like he might be this fella I knew in the Army, so I was wonderin' if anyone knows who he is."

"I saw him when Johnny ousted him," Riley said as he wiped the bar down using the same slimy rag with which he "cleaned" the glasses. "Don't know his name. He ain't a regular."

"Are you sure?" Will asked. "I heard he mighta come back the next night."

"Tuesday? Not that I noticed," Riley said, "and I'm right here near the front door. But then, there was all that mayhem after Johnny was shot."

"He would have come in before that," Will said.

Shaking his head, Riley said, "Finn might know. He was box-ing Tuesday night, but there ain't much goes on here that escapes him."

"Thanks, I'll go ask him."

"You'll have to wait till the match is over." Cocking his head toward the dance hall, Riley said, "That's him in the ring right now, fightin' Bulldog Cunigan."

They paused in the entrance to the dance hall, where scores of cheering and jeering onlookers stood gathered around a roped-off wooden platform in which Finn and his shorter but beefier opponent pounded each other with bare, blood-slicked fists. The clamor was deafening, the fight rawly savage.

"Attaboy, Southpaw!" someone yelled. "Teach 'im a lesson."

"Get him, Finn!" screeched a woman pressed right up against the ring, clutching the ropes: Pru. "Hammer him!"

Finn did hammer him, landing punch after punch to the head as Cunigan staggered backward. Sweat flew off the big Irishman as he pummeled his opponent, his face contorted in a feral gri-mace that made Nell shiver. With Cunigan now pinned against the ropes, Finn drove his left fist like a mallet into the poor fel-low's face, splitting his eyelid open and spraying blood.

Nell clutched her stomach, willing herself not to be sick.

"Nell." Will wrapped an arm around her and hustled her away from there. "Are you all right?" he asked, half-yelling to be heard above the din.

Expelling a shaky breath, she said, "He's an animal."

Will nodded. "It's not a sport with him, it's a kind of mania. You can see it in his eyes. Come—let's finish this up so I can get you out of here."

None of the bar girls or waitresses they questioned had seen Ben Shute return to Nabby's Tuesday night. By the time they got around to questioning Mother Nabby herself, the fight was over.

Nell was surprised it had lasted as long as it had, given the magnitude of the punishment Cunigan had absorbed.

"I don't see nothin' that happens out front, sittin' back here," Mother said as she puffed on her pipe. "But I do know Johnny had to boot out some cripple Monday."

"You didn't hear anything about him coming back?" Nell asked.

Mother shook her head. "Hey, listen, that flat's ready for you to move in any time you want. Blood's all cleaned up."

"Good to know. Is Denny Delaney around?" Will asked.

"Yeah, he's downstairs, sweepin' up," she said. "Or s'posed to be. Prob'ly down there with his nose in a book, lazy little scrap heap."

"A leg and an eye both?" Denny asked. They'd found him lying on a pallet in one of the empty "dance booths," reading *The Last of the Mohicans* by candlelight, his broom on the floor next to him. He'd panicked when they found him, fretting about getting punished for holing up down there, until they promised him they wouldn't tell.

Will said, "Yeah, he lost them at Fredericksburg."

"If he's the old acquaintance you're thinking of," Nell said.

"If he's the old acquaintance I'm thinking of."

Sitting up, Denny said, "I seen him. Saw him. I noticed him 'cause he was sittin' with Detective Cook Monday night, so I figured they must be friends. Then they left, but the gammy fella, he came back later and…" He looked away, shifting his jaw. "Him and Mary…you know."

"She brought him down here."

The boy nodded, picking at the rough woolen blanket with his fingers. "Johnny threw him out. He used to throw a lot of fellas out, the ones that…went with Mary. I think they musta got rough with her, some of them. I'd see bruises on her face afterwards, and little scrapes and cuts. Course, Johnny used to slap her around, too, sometimes, but I guess he wanted to be the only one to do it. I asked her once how come she put up with it, and she told me it was complicated, and there wouldn't be no way to make me understand."

"Did you ever see him again, after that night?" Nell asked. "The man Johnny threw out?"

"Sure, he came back the next night. I remember, 'cause it was right before Johnny got killed."

Nell and Will looked at each other.

"There was a fight goin' on," Denny said. "Not the first fight, between Finn and Davey Kerr. That only lasted two rounds before Finn knocked Kerr out. The second fight had started, but only just."

"The second fight," Will said. "Muldoon against McCann, right?"

"Right. It was the first round. I'd gone out back to, uh…" He glanced at Nell. "You know."

"Use the privy?" Will said.

Denny nodded. "When I come out, there's this fella just kinda standin' in the alleyway on the side there, lookin' down at something in his hand. It was dark, so at first I couldn't really tell what it was. He looked up, and I seen it was the fella from the night before that Johnny threw out. He had a top hat on, nice frock coat…He called me over, and when I got closer, I seen it was a newspaper he was holding."

"A newspaper?" Nell said.

"Yeah, all folded up real tight. He said he'd give me two bits if I'd give it to Johnny Cassidy, but I had to give it to him myself, not just leave it somewhere for him. I said sure. He gave me the two bits and the paper and left."

Will's grim expression echoed Nell's feelings. Chances were that newspaper was wrapped around a thousand dollars. Why would Ben Shute have paid Johnny the blackmail money, only to turn around and put a bullet in his head? This revelation boded well for Shute—but left Colin Cook as much a suspect as ever.

Nell said, "Did you get the chance to give Johnny the newspaper before he...?"

"Nah. Nah. It wasn't that long after that that he, uh, got shot."

"What did you do with it?" Will asked. "We'd like to see it if you still have it."

Denny frowned in concentration. "I dunno. I guess I musta left it in the—" He cut himself off, looked up at them, then quickly away. "Um...I guess I, uh, must have dropped it somewhere, you know, after Johnny was shot. It was so confusing and all, with everybody yelling and running around."

Nell crouched down so that she and the boy were at eye level. "Denny."

He looked at her; looked away.

"Where is it, Denny?"

"I...I dunno. I told you."

"You opened up the newspaper, didn't you?" she asked. "You saw what was inside."

"No. No, I swear. I just—"

"It's all right," Will said soothingly. "We're not cross with you. We just want to—"

"I don't have it!" Denny leapt to his feet. "I never even opened it up. I swear!"

"Denny, we think there's a great deal of money hidden inside that newspaper," Will said. "A thousand dollars."

The boy gaped at him.

"We know you're a good kid," Nell said. "You're like Detective Cook. You believe in doing the right thing. If you know where that money is, we'd like to give it back to the man who gave it to you."

"Who are you, really?" Denny demanded. "You ain't here to rent that flat, else you wouldn't know all this stuff. You wouldn't be askin' all these questions."

With a glance at Will, Nell said, "We're friends of Detective Cook's. Just like you."

"We know you lied to us," said Will. "You let us think you were upstairs when Johnny got killed, but you were down here."

Pushing between them, Denny said, "I gotta be getting back up there before they—"

Stopping the boy with a hand on his shoulder, Will said, "We know you saw Detective Cook standing over Johnny with his gun in his hand. And that Mary sent you upstairs."

"Finn woulda…" Denny clawed his hands through his hair. "I…I wasn't supposed to be down here."

"You saw what you saw," Will said, "yet you still don't think Cook killed Johnny?"

"He ain't a…" Denny grimaced, sighed. "He *isn't* a murderer. He didn't do it."

"Is that why you didn't you tell Constable Skinner that you saw him?" Nell asked. "Or was it that you didn't want to get in trouble for being down here?"

"They don't like me hanging out down here, reading."

"But they don't seem to mind you reading upstairs," Nell pointed out.

"Is it because Mary lived down here?" Will asked. "Because they didn't want you spending too much time near her flat?"

Denny looked back and forth between them, the blood rising in his cheeks.

Will said, "We know you used to watch her. We know that's why they put the padlock on the coal cellar door last year."

"We know that's why Finn broke your fingers and your nose," Nell said. "It seems like a pretty cruel punishment, if you ask me, worse than you deserved."

Denny shoved his hands in his pockets and muttered something that included the word "Mary."

"I'm sorry?" Nell said.

"I said even Mary thought so. She told me so. She asked me how come I started doin' it, and I told her I just found the hole one day when they sent me down to the coal cellar for booze, and I looked through it and there she was, sitting and playing cards all by herself. There was a candle on the table, and it made her hair look like a big red halo, like in those pictures of saints, and she looked kinda sad, but so pretty. Not in the way them other girls...those other girls are. With her, you know it's real, not just paint and stuff. And it was just...hard to stop lookin'. I told her it wasn't true, what they said about me watching her when she was...you know. When she didn't have her clothes on. I didn't do that."

"Never?" Will asked.

Looking down, the boy said, "Once, when I was watching, she started getting undressed for bed. I...watched till she was down to her, you know, her petticoats and stuff, and I reckon I... Well, part of me wanted to keep watching, but I knew if I did that, I'd have to confess it to Father Gannon, and I also knew it'd ruin everything, you know? It'd make it dirty, the watching. It had never been dirty before. So I left."

"And you told Mary all this?" Nell asked.

Denny nodded. "She said she was proud of me for leaving. She said she didn't like bein' watched at all, really, but she understood. She said I was just a boy with no girls around, no nice ones, anyway, and that boys get curious."

"Did she know you were sweet on her?" Nell asked gently.

Denny looked up sharply, as if to refute it, then lowered his gaze and mumbled, "I don't know. Maybe. She's pretty smart, and she knows a lot about, you know, people and stuff. She used to talk to me, after…after I got caught lookin' through the hole. About girls and stuff, and how I should get away from here before this place poisoned me. That's how she put it. She thought it would change me, being here. She wanted me to go back to school."

"You miss her, don't you?" Nell asked.

The boy nodded miserably. "It ain't gonna be the same around here. She's gone, Detective Cook's gone…"

"Cook is back, actually," Will said.

"He is?" Denny's look of delight evaporated as he took in their sober expressions. "They think he did it, huh?"

"He's been arrested," Will said. "They arraigned him yesterday afternoon, which means going to court to be charged with a crime. He was charged with murder and he pled not guilty. The judge denied bail, so he'll be held in jail until the trial."

"What's gonna happen then?" Denny asked.

"Well, we're hoping he'll be acquitted," Will said.

"Found not guilty," Nell explained.

"Do you think he will?" the boy asked as Nell and Will started up the stairs.

They paused, glanced at each other.

Nell said, "I promise you, Denny, we'll do everything we can to make sure that happens."

AFTER COMING BACK UPSTAIRS, NELL and Will re-interviewed everyone they'd spoken to before, trying to determine if anyone had seen a folded-up newspaper the night of the murder. Understandably, the question tended to inspire odd looks; who cared about a four day old newspaper?

"Prob'ly got tossed out with the trash," said Mother Nabby.

A thousand dollars, Nell thought, *carted away to wherever trash gets carted in this city.* It made her feel vaguely nauseated.

Finn Cassidy strode into the back room, still clad in his sweat-stained boxing pants, his bare chest speckled with blood. Pru was with him, carrying a red-smeared towel as if it were the victor's pennant.

"I heard you was lookin' for me durin' the fight," Finn said. "Riley said you was askin' 'bout that crip Johnny tossed outa here Monday night. I never seen him before or since. He a friend of yours?"

"I thought it might be this fella I knew during the war," Will said, "but it's probably—"

"There you are, you little pest," Mother growled.

They turned to find Denny standing outside the room, eyeing Finn warily. His face and clothes were stained with black dust, and he had something tucked under one arm.

"'Bout time you came back up here," Mother said. "What's that you got there?"

Denny held it up so she could see it, but he was looking at Nell and Will. "J-just a newspaper."

CHAPTER SEVENTEN

INN SNATCHED THE NEWSPAPER OUT of Denny's hand. "You were readin' downstairs again?"

"He does it all the time," Pru said as she wiped the towel over Finn's back and shoulders.

Making a fist, Finn said, "I'm thinkin' maybe he needs a little remindin' about—"

"It's *my* newspaper," Will said as he grabbed it from Finn. "I've been looking for it. Thanks, Denny. You're a good kid."

"Wait till you know him a little better," Pru sneered. "He's a worthless little rat if ever there was one."

Finn swatted her away as she reached up to dab his face with the towel. "Would you cut that out? I can't hardly breathe with you crawlin' all over me like that."

"Speakin' of rats," Mother said, "Skinner stopped by just now to collect his weekly take. He said they caught that state cop that shot Johnny Cassidy. You know," she said to Nell and Will, "the fella that used to live in the room you're rentin'? He said they're holdin' the bastard without bail. Said he's gonna swing fer sure."

"Good riddance. Murderin' son of a bitch." Finn spat on the floor. "May he roast in Hell."

Pru turned, hands on hips, to glare at Denny. "What the hell are *you* starin' at? Finn, do you see how this little quat is lookin' at you?"

Indeed, there was no mistaking the fury that Denny was leveling at Finn. His jaw got that same hard thrust to it that Will's did, Nell noticed.

"You got some nerve, lookin' at me that way," Finn said.

"Yeah," Denny said in a voice that shook as much with anger, it seemed to Nell, as with fear, "well, *you* got some nerve, callin' Detective Cook a murderer when it was you that put that bullet in Johnny's head."

Finn stared at Denny, the whites showing all around his irises. "What did you say?" he asked in a strained near-whisper.

Pru's sloppily rouged mouth was hanging open. "Why, you little—"

"You killed your own brother," Denny said shakily. "If anybody's gonna roast in Hell, I reckon it'll be—"

Finn lunged for him, hauling back with his fist. Will reacted in a blur, blocking the punch and landing one of his own to Finn's jaw.

"Get him, Finn!" Pru screamed. "He can't fight! He's a fairy! Knock him out!"

"Pru!" hollered Mother as the two men traded punches. "Go fetch Skinner. He just left. Look next door."

Nell executed a swift sign of the cross as Pru ran off, praying that Will's long arms and semi-dormant boxing skills would be a match for the vicious, brawny Irishman. She flinched every time Finn's fist slammed into Will, wondering how he could take the abuse—although Will's punches actually connected more often, due to his quickness as his reach. One of those punches whipped Finn's head around and sent him flying into the wall. He slid down until he was sitting with his legs splayed and his head nodding forward, like some monstrous, half-naked rag doll, eyes unfocused, face battered, blood trickling from his mouth.

"Holy gee," Denny said, staring in awe at the felled giant.

"Are you all right, Will?" Nell asked. He had a purpling knot on his forehead and a pretty bad scrape on his cheekbone, and she knew he'd taken some shots to the midsection.

He nodded, dragging his hair off his forehead and straightening his frock coat. In a slightly winded voice—his own, reassuringly familiar British-accented voice—he said, "I'd forgotten what splendid exercise that is."

"You English?" Mother asked.

"Guilty."

Seemingly unperturbed at having been misled up till now, she said, "You need to be boxing for me. Tuesdays and Saturdays. It's a four-dollar purse plus some of what changes hands here on fight night. We'll call you 'Sir Something' or 'Lord Something,' pit the Brit against the mick. The crowd'll love it. You'll have to take a fall now and then, but you'll find it's worth your while."

"That's quite an offer, Mother. I've always secretly yearned for a title. But I'm afraid it won't be possible."

"We'll make it a five dollar purse, and I'll throw in the chicken house for free."

"A chicken house, too? That *is* tempting."

"It's all yours," Mother said, "soon as I can get Finn out of there."

The insensate boxer fluttered his eyes and mumbled something when he heard his name, then went limp again.

"If what Denny says is true," Nell said, "the Commonwealth of Massachusetts will be taking responsibility for Finn's accommodations from now on."

"That kid don't know nothin'," Mother said contemptuously as she stuffed tobacco into her pipe. "He don't like Finn, is all. Two of them just don't get along."

Nell said, "I don't suppose that would have anything to do with Finn breaking his nose and his fingers."

"He got off easy," Mother said. "He was peekin' into Mary and Johnny's flat. I had to put a padlock on the coal cellar door to stop him from gettin' in there."

"I don't think it worked," Nell said, exchanging a little smile with Denny.

"What do you mean?" Mother asked.

Denny nodded, as if to give her permission to divulge what she'd just figured out.

"He's been getting in through the coal chute," Nell said. "Look at him, he's got coal dust all over him."

"You little Peeping Tom," Mother snarled.

"I wasn't peeping," Denny said. "Not like you mean. After the lock was put on the door to the coal cellar, I didn't go in there for a long time—three, four months, anyway. But then one day I was out in the back yard and I heard Mary cry out like she'd been hit. I saw the coal chute, and I thought maybe I was just skinny enough to get through, and I was. I slipped through and landed in the coal crib—the coal broke my fall. So then I looked through the hole and I saw Mary sittin' with her head in her hands, but Johnny'd already left. I watched her for a couple of minutes just to make sure she was all right, and then I climbed back out through the chute."

"And you continued getting in that way?" Will asked.

"Only when I thought Mary might, you know, need some help. Like if Johnny started drinkin' and got in one of his moods and headed down there. I told her I wouldn't watch her like I used to, and I didn't."

Scowling at Denny, Mother said, "How a man chooses to keep his woman in line is his business, and nobody else's. If Finn could do it right now, I'd have him bust every bone in that sawed off little body of yours. As it is, you can find someplace else to lay your head from now on. I don't want to see you here when I come in tomorrow."

"Yeah, I figured," Denny said.

"You knew there would be consequences if Mother and Finn found out what you've been doing," Will told the boy, "yet you've admitted to it anyway."

"It's 'cause of Detective Cook," he said. "I woulda 'fessed up sooner, but I kept thinkin' the cops would figure out it was really

Finn that killed Johnny, and they wouldn't have to hear it from me."

"Because then everyone would find out you'd continued peeking into Mary and Johnny's flat even after the coal cellar door was locked," Nell said. "I take it that's how you know it was Finn."

Denny said, "I reckoned it'd be bad enough, havin' Mother toss me back out onto the street. If Finn got his hands on me, I'd have been lucky just to get busted up. But now Cook's in jail, and he might hang if I don't tell what I know. He wouldn't let that happen to me if he could help it, so I can't let it happen to him."

"What *do* you know?" Nell asked. "Why don't you start with the newspaper? How did it get in the coal cellar? I take it that's where you got it from just now."

"Yeah, when you asked me about it downstairs, I realized that's where I musta left it. I didn't really think about it, 'cause I figured it was just a newspaper, and Johnny was supposed to get it, but he was dead."

"Why did you go down there in the first place?" Will asked. "Were you concerned about Mary?"

"Yeah, but not because of Johnny. It was him." Denny cocked his head toward Finn, lolling against the wall. "I was around the side of the house, in the alleyway. It was right after that crippled fella gave me that." He nodded toward the folded newspaper in Will's hand. "I was standing there wondering what Johnny wanted with a newspaper, seeing as how he could barely read, when I heard Finn sayin' Mary's name. So I peeked around the side of the house, and there was Finn, still in his boxing pants, like now. His match was over, and they'd started the second one. He was knockin' on the door to Mary and Johnny's flat, but if Mary was saying anything, I couldn't hear her. He kept saying, 'Let me in, Mary. I just want to talk.' That kind of thing."

"Was he in the habit of visiting her alone?" Will asked.

"Not that I knew," Denny said. "Johnny was upstairs taking bets on the second match, which is probably why Finn picked that time to go see her. Finally she kinda cracked the door open a little and said something I couldn't hear. She started to close it again, but Finn kicked it back open."

"Kicked it?" Will said.

"Yeah, and Mary kind of yelped, so I think it may have hit her, or maybe she was just scared. Finn went in, and I heard him say, 'Shut your mouth' before he closed the door behind him."

"So that's when you slipped down through the coal chute," Nell said.

"I was worried about her."

"Fight over?" It was Charlie Skinner, with Pru in tow, strutting into the room swinging his truncheon. Taking in the slowly rousing Finn with a low whistle, he said, "I reckon so."

"Finn!" Pru threw herself on Finn. "What'd he do to you?"

Skinner prodded Finn in the gut with his truncheon. "Whose handiwork is this?"

"His." Mother pointed to Will. "I'm trying to talk him into getting into the ring. I never seen anybody K.O. Finn Cassidy— not in half a minute, anyways."

Skinner turned, his face twisting in vexation as he noticed Nell and Will for the first time. "You two. God help me! If you're mixed up in this, I don't want nothin' to do with it."

"Finn. Darlin'." Pru patted her beloved's cheek, shook his shoulders. Turning to Will with rage in her eyes, she said, "You killed him, you goddamned fairy."

"'Felled by a fairy,'" Will mused. "Now, there's a fitting epitaph for Finn Cassidy."

Resting a hand on Denny's shoulder, Nell told Skinner, "This boy is an eyewitness to the murder. He was watching through a spy hole Tuesday night when Finn paid a visit to Mary. He'd forced his way into the flat."

Giving Finn a rough shake, Pru said, "Finn—wake up. The kid's tellin' tales about you."

Finn blinked his eyes open and pushed Pru's hands away, grumbling, "Get *off* me. I *told* you."

"I'm not tellin' tales," Denny said. "I saw what I saw, and I heard what I heard."

"Oh, yeah?" Skinner said with a dubious little smirk. "So what'd you see and hear, then?"

"Finn told Mary that him and Pru had been talkin' about her earlier, before the fight. Pru had told him he should stop mooning over Mary, 'cause she wasn't the sweet young thing she pretended to be—in fact, she was lifting her skirts for a cop and payin' her—Pru—to keep it quiet, and the only reason she was telling Finn about it was she'd rather have him than the money. He said, 'She thinks she's in love with me, but I expect I can do better than a poxy little piece like that.'"

"He did not! He couldn't of." Pru spun on Finn in incredulous outrage. "Did you say that?"

"Huh?"

She slapped his face, hard. *"Did you?"*

"Ow!" Finn sat up, rubbing his jaw. "What's got into you, you crazy little bitch?"

Pru bolted to her feet with a shriek of outrage, lifted her skirts, and kicked Finn in the stomach, whereupon he doubled over, sputtering a litany of vile curses. He tried to kick her back, but she sidestepped him nimbly.

"You bitch," he groaned, endeavoring somewhat unsteadily to raise himself up off the floor.

"Poxy?" She dealt him another, more powerful kick, this one aimed somewhat lower than the first. *"Poxy?"* Finn collapsed with a roar that degenerated into a whimper, clutching his groin as he curled up into a ball.

"You should put *her* in the ring," Skinner told Mother.

"What was Mary's reaction to what Finn said?" Nell asked Denny.

"She said it wasn't true, about her and Cook, but Finn didn't believe her. He said she was worse than whores like Pru, 'cause at least they're honest about what they are. He said she'd been teasing him, leading him on. She said she hadn't, neither. She said she'd told him she didn't feel that way about him, and that she wouldn't have slipped around on Johnny even if she did, but that just got him madder. He said she *had* been slippin' around on Johnny, just not with him, and that she'd played him like a sucker, and he'd fallen for it, and that was why he'd been askin' her to run away with him and get hitched, but he wasn't gonna ask her no more, 'cause men like him didn't marry 'loose baggage' like her. He said…he said, 'This is all you're good for,' and he, um…he grabbed her…where he shouldn't have, and pushed her onto the bed, and started pulling at her clothes."

"Did she scream?" Nell asked.

"Or did it seem like it was what she wanted all along?" Skinner sneered.

"She screamed," Denny told the constable, in a tone that brooked no quarrel. "But with the fight goin' on upstairs, nobody coulda heard her. He said, 'You did it with Cook, why not me?' She hit him, so he punched her in the face—hard."

Will made a sound of disgust.

"Detective Cook told me it was the right side of Mary's face that was bloodied," Nell said. "That would make sense, given that Finn is left-handed."

Denny said, "I jumped down from the coal crib and started feelin' around in the dark for the shovel, and that's when I heard the door to the flat open."

"The outside door?" Will asked. "Or—"

"No, the inside one, the one that's next to the coal room door. And then I heard Johnny kickin' up a row, and Mary telling him to put away his gun—beggin' him, really. So I jumped back up on the coal crib to look through the hole, and I seen the two of 'em, Johnny and Finn, fightin', but up close. Not like in the ring, where they're throwing punches, but...you know, like they're wrestling. And then Finn pushed Johnny real hard, onto this old sea chest they got in there. And he raised his hand—Finn did—and I seen he'd gotten the gun away from Johnny. Johnny said, 'I'll kill you,' and he kind of lunged at Finn, and..." Denny shook his head.

"Finn pulled the trigger," Will finished.

"You're putting words in the boy's mouth," Skinner said.

"He pulled the trigger," Denny said. "I seen the flash and I heard the crack, and Johnny kind of...flew back against the chest and then fell on the floor. His head...Th-there was blood..."

"We know," Nell said softly. "Where was Mary when this was happening?"

"She was crouched down in the corner, shakin' like a rabbit. She's sayin', 'Oh, my God, oh, my God, your own brother...' Finn's starin' down at Johnny like he ain't sure what just happened. He starts screamin' at Mary to shut up. He pointed the gun at her and said it was all her fault. I think...He had his back to me, but I think he mighta been cryin'. But he was screamin', too. I could see the gun, and it was shakin' in his hand. He told her to get lost. He said 'You stick around, or tell a soul what happened here, you're dead.' And then he started, kind of, pacin' around the room, and he said, 'No, I gotta take care of you, too, 'cause you'll talk, I know you'll talk.' And he aimed the gun at her again, so I grabbed the shovel and went out and banged on the door of the flat and yelled somethin' about how Mother was lookin' for Mary and she wanted her right away, and like that. And I heard him tell her to keep her mouth shut if she knew what was good for her, and then I heard the outside door open. It's got these real rusty hinges, so it makes a lot of noise. So I went in, and—"

"You went into the flat?" Will asked.

"Yeah, and she was still in the corner, but Finn was gone. I heard him runnin' up the stairs. Mary jumped up and started packin' her things, real quick. I told her what I saw, and she said 'Don't say a word, Denny, or you'll end up dead, too.' Coupla minutes later, Detective Cook came in the back way. He saw Johnny layin' there dead and pulled his gun. He asked Mary who did it, but she wouldn't tell him. She yelled at me to go upstairs and make like I was never down there. So I did."

"After making sure Detective Cook would take care of Mary," Nell said.

"Well, sure," Denny said, as if it were a given. "Wasn't long before all hell broke loose. I was standin' at the top of the basement stairs, wonderin' what to do, when I heard Pru raisin' a racket downstairs. She comes runnin' up, screamin' murder. Mother sent me for the cops. I found *him* a couple of blocks away—" the boy pointed to Skinner "—and brung him back. As God is my witness, that's exactly the way it happened."

"We'll see about that." Skinner turned to Finn, still curled up on the floor, and nudged him with his boot. "Hey, Cassidy. *Cassidy*. D'you hear what this kid…? Cassidy?"

Finn Cassidy's shoulders were shaking. He turned his head; his face was wet with tears. "I didn't mean to. It was her fault. She… she…Oh, God…I'm sorry, Johnny. God help me, I'm so sorry."

Skinner regarded the prostrate man in grave silence, then let out a long, deeply crestfallen sigh. "Shit."

"Cook! Hey, Cook!" Skinner bellowed later that night as he hammered his truncheon on the grillwork of Detective Cook's holding cell at the Division Eight station house. "Wake up. Your pals are here to spring you."

Cook, who'd been dozing on a sunken little cot against the back wall, sat up groggily, blinking at Nell and Will. His hair was in disarray, his chimney sweep attire rumpled; a prickly growth of beard showed through the remnants of soot still darkening his face, although it appeared he'd tried to wipe most of it off. He put Nell in mind of a bear just rousing from his winter hibernation.

"Spring me?" Cook said. "You're joking."

"Unfortunately," the constable said, "I'm dead serious." It *was* unfortunate for Skinner, whose "Paddy captain," a fellow named Quinn, had berated him within Nell and Will's hearing about his suspicious mishandling of this case. Nell couldn't help recalling, during this dressing down, Skinner's comment about his superiors regarding him as a "stray cat they'd like to drown."

Cook's incredulous gaze came to rest on Nell; he smiled slowly. "Miss Sweeney, you will never cease to astonish me."

"Yeah, she's a shrewd little thing," Skinner said, "but then so are you, eh, Cook? You clever micks always seem to rise up outa the sewage smellin' like clover."

"Careful, Constable," Nell warned. "Remember what your captain told you. One more insolent comment to or about Detective Cook, and you're off the force."

"Really?" Cook said.

"It surprises you that Captain *Quinn* takes your side? Maybe you ain't as clever as I thought." Choosing a key from the massive ring the guard had given him, Skinner unlocked the iron-barred door and swung it open with a raspy squeal. "Out you go," he said, gesturing with the truncheon. "We need this cell for Finn Cassidy."

"Cassidy?" Cook said as he hauled himself up off the cot, rubbing the small of his back. "Really?" he asked Nell.

"We'll fill you in later," Nell said. "For now, let's just get you back home to Mrs. Cook."

As the big detective lumbered through the door, Skinner said, with an uneasy little grin, "Gotta admit, Detective, you looked guilty as sin. No harm done, though, really."

Turning the great wall of his back to Skinner as he dusted off his coat and finger-combed his hair, Cook said tightly, "Tell that to my wife. She almost lost the baby, frettin' over whether you were gonna get me hanged."

"Did she, now? Well, that old country soil's pretty fruitful, I hear. If one sprout don't come up—" Skinner actually winked, the dog "—it'd give you another chance to plant a new one, eh?"

Cook wheeled around in a blur, driving a fist the size of a cannonball into the constable's head. Before Nell could blink in reaction, Skinner lay sprawled on the floor, his hat rolling off in one direction, truncheon clattering away in another. He yowled in shock and pain, hands covering his bruised face.

"Nice work, detective," said Will as he regarded the writhing constable with amused dispassion. Leaning over for a closer look, he added, in a tone of mild disappointment, "It would appear that his jaw's still intact."

"I held back," said Cook as he rubbed his reddened knuckles. "Wanted him to be able to operate that jaw."

"Why, for pity's sake?"

Will got his answer when several other cops, including Captain Quinn, came rushing to see what all the commotion was about.

"What happened here?" Quinn demanded.

"I believe Constable Skinner may have tripped over that," Nell said, pointing to his truncheon, "and taken a spill."

"You lying bitch!" screamed the red-faced Skinner as he raised himself up on an elbow. Pointing a quivering finger at Detective

Cook, he said, "That goddamn bogtrotter punched me!" He went on to hurl at his assailant a stream of invective as vile as Nell had ever heard, and then some, while Cook stood by with a self-satisfied little smile.

Looking pretty satisfied himself, the lieutenant said, "Skinner, what did I tell you not ten minutes ago about insulting Detective Cook?"

"But...but he—"

"Collect your things and leave," Quinn said. "You're no longer a member of this department."

"Nice work, indeed, detective," Nell whispered as they turned to leave.

CHAPTER EIGHTEEN

THE SUBSTANCE OF THINGS HOPED for.

The phrase drifted in and out of Nell's mind as she lay awake the following night, listening to the faint tick...tick...tick of the grandfather clock downstairs, punctuated by an occasional creak from the bed on the other side of the wall. Will had insisted on leaving the connecting door open as before, reasoning that Charlie Skinner was no less of a threat for having been sacked; probably more so.

Substance. A word of consequence, hefty as an old pair of boots...

Hope. Light as a breath, soft as a heartbeat...

The distant clock proclaimed midnight with a succession of stately, muffled gongs. Nell had been lying in this bed trying to get to sleep for over an hour and a half. This time, her sleeplessness couldn't be blamed on the heat, for it was pleasant enough tonight to need her quilt; nor was it the product of fear, for she trusted Will to protect her if need be.

Her wakefulness stemmed from the sermon Martin had delivered at King's Chapel this morning, which Nell and Will had gone to hear, and which she couldn't seem to stop ruminating on. "The Substance of Things Hoped For" was a discourse on the foundations of faith, beautifully expressed. Martin had truly found his calling. He'd always been wise beyond his years, compassionate, articulate...a winning combination for a man of the cloth. Nell had found herself not just inspired, but deeply moved by his observations on life and devotion, many of which seemed to speak directly to her circumstances.

Afterward, Nell and Will had chatted with the handsome new reverend on the front steps of the church. Martin looked so at home in his clerical robes, despite his youth. He told them he'd be leaving tomorrow for four weeks on the Cape before launching into his new pastoral duties, taking his little coal box buggy instead of the train, which he hated. Will suggested that Nell accompany Martin rather than traveling alone, which made him nervous given recent events, so it was arranged; Martin told her he'd come by for her at seven tomorrow morning.

Excusing himself to Nell, Will had taken his brother out of earshot for a brief, private conversation. Nell had watched surreptitiously as they spoke, with Will doing most of the talking. Whatever he'd said had seemed quite troubling to Martin; he'd grabbed Will's shoulders, his expression earnest, imploring. Will had glanced at Nell, then shaken his head. He took something out of his vest pocket—it was too small for Nell to make out—and pressed it into Martin's hand, then hugged him tight. It was a rare display of emotion for Will Hewitt. Nell couldn't help but wonder what had transpired between the brothers, but of course it wouldn't do to ask.

After lunching at the Parker House, Nell and Will had returned home to find a note from the Cooks, inviting them to pay an afternoon call. When they arrived at the brick townhouse on Fayette Street, they found not just Chloe's friend Lily Booth there, but Denny Delaney as well.

Detective Cook, as it turned out, had gone to Nabby's early that morning in search of Denny, only to be told he'd packed his paltry belongings and left during the night, unwilling to remain one moment longer under the roof of someone who didn't want him there. Cook had found him at St. Stephen's, asleep in a rear pew during early mass. The boy had allowed Cook to bring him home and feed him, after the detective had explained that it was merely a gesture of thanks for coming forward to clear his name, but he'd drawn the line at Cook's offer, once again, for him to live there and attend Boston College High School. That would be crossing the line, he'd said, from gratitude to charity.

As they were enjoying a light afternoon repast of tea and apple fritters—made by Lily, since Chloe, although much improved, wasn't moving from her couch in the front parlor—Ebenezer Shute came by. Detective Cook, to whom Will had entrusted the newspaper-wrapped thousand dollars, tried to return it to Shute, who refused to take it. Instead, he bequeathed it to Denny, explaining that it was part of his reward for having exonerated both him and Colin Cook, despite the risk to himself. Predictably, Denny's outsized pride got in the way, and he tried to reject the money as a handout, obliging everyone present to spend most of the remaining afternoon explaining the difference between money that was donated because of poverty and that which was earned.

That concept having sunk in, Denny was in a more receptive frame of mind by the time Shute got around to the second part of his reward: an education at Georgetown Prep, the Jesuit boarding school where Shute's brother—who owed him a favor—was headmaster, plus college tuition once he graduated. This time, Denny offered only the most cursory objection before gratefully accepting the offer. He spent the rest of the afternoon in a giddy daze of anticipation.

At one point during the afternoon, Nell noticed that Will wasn't there. Chloe told her he'd stepped out to run an errand. When he came back and Nell asked him where he'd gone, he called her a "meddling duchess" and changed the subject. Then, after they returned home following dinner at Jacob Wirth's, he sequestered himself behind the closed door of his father's library for almost an hour. When he emerged, she didn't ask what he'd been doing in there, knowing he'd just tease her about nosiness again. In any event, he didn't owe her an accounting of his time. She wasn't his wife, or anything close to it.

The substance of things hoped for.

Curled up on her side, Nell closed her eyes, trying to coax her racing mind to surrender to sleep.

The substance of things…

Things hoped for…

Hoped For…

Things—

The sound was soft, almost imperceptible, a papery whisper against the linen pillowcase behind her. Nell would never have heard it had it not been so close, mere inches from her head.

She lay on her side, facing away from the door on the lefthand side of the bed. As far as she could tell, something had just been placed upon the righthand pillow.

Nell waited, eyes closed, heart drumming, for an interminable minute, until she heard the bed in the adjacent room groan slightly as Will lay back down. She wouldn't have guessed that a man his size could move so quietly.

She opened her eyes and waited another few minutes, until the sounds of him shifting about on the bed had faded away, to sit up and look behind her. A nearly full moon shone through the sheer curtains, casting the room in a kind of radiant twilight, so she had no trouble seeing the envelope lying in the middle of the pillow. She lifted it, finding it weighty, and held it close to her face to make out what was written on the front in Will's angular, masculine hand: *Nell.*

Rising from the bed slowly and silently, so as not to draw Will's attention, Nell brought the envelope over to a window that was brighter than the rest, owing to the street lamp directly below. She broke the wax seal and unfolded three sheets of thick ivory vellum engraved *148 Tremont Street, Boston, Massachusetts:*

August Hewitt's writing paper, which he kept in a neat stack on his library desk.

10 July 1870

My dearest Nell,

Forgive this cowardly letter, I beg you. Some things are more easily written than spoken aloud.

I won't be here when you awaken. Yesterday afternoon, when I stepped out during our visit with the Cooks, it was for two purposes— first, to wire President Grant my acceptance of the appointment as field surgeon to Ambassador Washburne, and second, to book passage to France. It happened that there was one remaining stateroom available on the Melita, *which departs tomorrow morning, so I reserved it. I must leave here before dawn to gather my effects in order to be at Constitution Wharf when the ship boards.*

By the time I arrive in Paris, France will in all likelihood be embroiled in war with Prussia. My duties are as yet undefined. All I know for certain is that I am to serve the ambassador in whatever capacity he requires. Given his specific request for a surgeon with wartime experience, and his own political sympathies, I suspect that I am to provide medical services to Napoleon's army on the field of battle. There is no explicit term to my service, and of course, no telling how long the fighting will last. It is possible, likely even, that I could be gone for years.

You will wonder why I've chosen this course, rather than the more comfortable alternative of teaching at Harvard. We have reached a juncture in the path of our acquaintance, you and I, from whence we cannot continue as before, strolling along side by side with no particular destination in mind, at least none of which we dare speak. If this turn of events grieves me, I have only myself to blame. Our friendship had its parameters, which you, in your wisdom, always respected, and which I, as is my nature, ultimately overstepped.

I am a far better man for having known you, Nell, but I am ultimately a selfish man, or I would never have imposed upon your tender nature as I did at the railroad station last January. The fault was entirely mine, but the cost, I regret to say, is one which we both must bear.

I had promised you, when I asked for that kiss, that we would go on afterward as before. Were I a stronger man, perhaps I could simply lift my chin and do so, but I think we both know that my fortitude has its limits. Did I not crave relief from pain—all manner of pain, not just the physical variety—I would never have wasted all those years in the numbing embrace of Morphia.

Sooner or later, I will weaken and contrive to violate, once more, the boundaries of our friendship. Whether you rebuff me or indulge me, the result will be the same. I will inevitably press you for more, you will grow to resent me, and the priceless attachment that has evolved between us these past years will be irreparably spoiled.

Having given the matter much consideration, I have arrived at the sad conviction that the time has come for us to step apart. It would be far better, for both our sakes, to withdraw from one another now, than to permit what we've shared to decay into something bitter and complicated. When people ask about our presumed engagement, simply tell them that you ended it over my gambling, aimlessness, and various other bad habits and defects of character; no one will question that.

Give Gracie a kiss for me. Tell her how sorry I am not to have seen her before I left, and that I will write to her when the opportunity presents itself.

Please do forgive the abruptness of my departure, and don't, I implore you, attempt to come to the wharf to see me off. I haven't the backbone for it, and in fact I've asked Martin to keep you away. He'll be coming to the house around 5:00 tomorrow morning to keep *watch over you after I leave. Yesterday after church I gave him the spare key to my house so that he can live there when he returns from the Cape next month.*

It has taken all my strength of will to commit these words to paper, Nell, and it will take even more to leave this letter on your pillow tonight. You befriended me when I was in dire need a friend, you saved me when I needed a savior. Your presence in my life has shone a light upon my soul that will never be extinguished. For that precious gift, I shall forever be in your debt.

Yours in undying affection,
Will

Nell could barely breathe by the time she finished the letter. It felt as if there were a giant iron clamp around her chest, squeezing, squeezing…

She re-read the letter through a sheen of tears, sorting it all out in her mind—the things he'd said, and hadn't said, the nuances and implications. Unmentioned was her marriage to Duncan, yet Nell couldn't help but suspect that, if she could only free herself from it, Will would have chosen to remain in Boston rather than risk his life in a war that meant nothing to him.

She refolded the letter and crawled back into bed, shivering in her thin night shift, although the breeze fluttering the curtains was a mild one. *Don't cry,* she told herself even as the tears pooling in her eyes spilled down her cheeks. She scrubbed them away, thinking, *Don't cry. He'll hear. He's trying to be strong. So must you.*

She tried to draw a calming breath, but it snagged in her throat, emerging as a sob that she muffled by turning her face to the pillow. Another wrenched itself out of her, and another, and another, silent but wracking.

"Nell."

She felt the mattress dip with his weight. He lowered himself atop the quilt behind her, banding an arm around her waist as he tucked his long body, clad in loose linen drawers, against hers.

"I'm sorry," he whispered, his breath hot in her hair, his arm tightening around her. "I'm sorry, Nell."

He snugged himself closer, draping his outside leg protectively around hers as he murmured things she couldn't hear. As she absorbed his warmth, his tenderness, her crying ebbed, leaving her limp in his arms. She loosed a hand from the bedcovers to lace her fingers with his. It was the kind of thing lovers did, she realized, but she was beyond caring about appearances and repercussions.

She was losing him yet again—to a war this time.

"W-will it—" Her voice caught. "Will it be like…like it was during the War Between the States, where battle surgeons aren't supposed to be fired upon?"

He took his time answering. "I don't know."

She closed her eyes and gripped his hand harder, feeling a terrible, black foreboding. "Don't go."

He nuzzled her head, sighed. "I've given the president my word. It can't be taken back."

She shook her head, her eyes stinging with fresh tears. "I hate this."

Propping himself up on an arm, Will eased Nell onto her back and brushed away the hair that clung to her damp face. The moonlight shadowed his eyes and silvered his skin, throwing the bruise and scrape on his face into sharp contrast. She breathed in his familiar scent, trying to store it away in her memory—Bay Rum, warm skin, and a hint of tobacco; he must have smoked a cigarette, probably while he was in his father's library writing that letter.

He blotted her face with the edge of the sheet, then lowered his head until his forehead rested against hers. She heard him swallow. A hot little droplet struck her eyelid and trickled down the side of her face.

She freed both arms from the quilt and gathered him to her, their mouths meeting as naturally, as ardently, as if they'd done so a thousand times and not just once, during another anguished parting half a year before. The kiss stole her breath, her senses. The world, with all its conventions and expectations, dissolved away, leaving just the two of them alone in this room, this bed.

"I should go," he said hoarsely, his hands tangled in her hair.

"No, don't." The softspoken plea resonated between them before she even realized she'd spoken.

Will searched her gaze, his eyes dark and shimmering.

Nell drew in a breath, willing herself to take it back, to bow to her mind and not her heart, to do the right thing, the prudent thing, but when the air left her lungs, it emerged in a whispered, heartfelt, "Stay."